PASSERBY: A PSYCHOLOGICAL THRILLER

BRITNEY KING

ALSO BY BRITNEY KING

Passerby

Kill Me Tomorrow

Savage Row

The Book Doctor

Kill, Sleep, Repeat

Room 553

HER

The Social Affair | Book One

The Replacement Wife | Book Two

Speak of the Devil | Book Three

Water Under The Bridge | Book One

Dead In The Water | Book Two

Come Hell or High Water | Book Three

Bedrock | Book One

Breaking Bedrock | Book Two

Beyond Bedrock | Book Three

Around The Bend

Somewhere With You | Book One

Anywhere With You | Book Two

COPYRIGHT

Hot Banana Press
Cover Design by Britney King LLC
Cover Image by Clayton Bunn & Elijah O'Donnell
Copy Editing by Librum Artis
Proofread by Proofreading by the Page

First Edition: 2021
ISBN 13: 9798538696901
ISBN 10: 9798538696

britneyking.com

For you.

PASSERBY

BRITNEY KING

" There are only two tragedies in life: one is not getting what one wants, and the other is getting it. **"** - Oscar Wilde

PROLOGUE

Now

This is not a job for an amateur. That much is obvious by the way my heart has lodged itself in my throat. I cover my mouth, partly because I'm in shock, partly because it will keep me from screaming. As tears prick my eyes, I bite down on my tongue in an attempt to keep them at bay. I am not a crier.

I push the door open further and enter the room. *Small hinges move heavy doors.* It's something my father used to say. I wish he were here now. He would know what to do.

My focus suddenly becomes very narrow, very clear. I stand frozen in place until I realize I ought to close the door behind me. I lock it for good measure, even though every fiber of my being is telling me to get out. *Turn around and run. Don't look back.*

Spoiler alert, that's not what I do.

I take another step forward.

The floor creaks underfoot as I move toward the desk, causing my heart to lurch further into my throat. After flipping on the lamp, I cross the room carefully. I reach for the curtains then realize I probably shouldn't. Guests have already begun trickling into the garden, and while I'm on the second floor, people have a way of seeing everything these days.

Not me, unfortunately. I should have checked this room earlier. Back when I sensed something was wrong. Back when I felt someone watching me. The times I heard funny noises.

I scan the room for answers, though it's pretty obvious what has happened. A double murder. That, or a murder-suicide. One way or the other, I have two bodies on my hands. Two bodies I have to get rid of and quick. Nothing spoils a party faster than a dead body. Two dead bodies and things go downhill twice as fast.

I hope you'll forgive my facetiousness. I'm awkward in situations that are outside of my control. But then again, I'm awkward most of the time.

The alarm clock on the nightstand catches my attention as it blinks on and off, flashing red, indicating that someone has unplugged it and plugged it back in. It reads 2:00 p.m.

I wish it was 2:00 p.m. I slide my phone from my back pocket and check the time. I have exactly twenty-seven minutes.

I can do this.

I have to do this.

There's a lot riding on me doing this.

I remind myself that I am not an amateur. I know how to get blood out of carpet, sheets, and fancy dresses. You name it, I'm sure I've tried it. I know how to scrub walls meticulously, but also carefully, so as not to rub the paint off. I know that when it comes to flooring, when a job is too big—like, say, this one—you don't bother trying to scrub, you simply cut swatches of carpet out. It never looks quite right, even if you manage to find a suitable match, but a piece of furniture, carefully placed, or a rug, will take care of that.

Here, I don't know. There's an awful lot of blood. The plush carpet that was just installed last January? Toast. I'm guessing drywall will have to be removed. One thing is for sure, someone in this room fought like hell. I wonder which of them it was. Was it both?

I clench my fists and then stretch my fingers. The mattress is a goner, for sure. I can't afford this. Although, there isn't time to think about that now. This requires a quick fix, a Band-Aid, *anything* that will buy me some time. Not enough time to call professionals, although that's certainly what I'd prefer.

Like The Rolling Stones said: You can't always get what you want.

And anyway, I can't afford professionals, either.

I know what you're thinking. You're thinking, I could do what most people in my shoes would do. I could call the police.

Trust me, that's probably the least affordable option.

There are lives at stake, and livelihoods, which are sometimes one and the same, more so than you'd think.

So here I am, standing over two dead bodies, surveying the blood splatter, wondering if I'll ever be able to find wallpaper this pretty again. It's like two paths diverged in a wood. I know this isn't a Robert Frost poem, but bear with me, it's my favorite, and at this moment, my mind is going to strange places. It's the shock, a protective mechanism. You wouldn't believe the things our brains and our bodies can do. They can perform miraculous feats in the name of preservation.

If only it had worked for these two.

Anyway, two paths diverged in a wood...and here I am, staring down both of them. Only, I know what's in store; I know where they lead. Path number one is the right choice, of course. The obvious choice. The good choice. The moral high ground. Path number two is the choice only a desperate person would make. A fool's trip. One that leads to nowhere good. And yet...*what choice do I have?*

I could try to explain myself. But you wouldn't understand. No one can possibly understand. Not until they've walked a mile in my shoes, and believe me, they wouldn't want that, either. My shoes are currently taking on blood faster than the *Titanic* took on water.

Deep breath in. Deep breath out.

I can do this.

I have to do this.

I wring my hands out, wiping my sweaty palms on my shorts. Sweat slides down my spine. *No, not a job for an amateur at all.*

Thankfully, I've read up on the bio-recovery industry. Most people refer to it as crime scene cleanup—biohazard remediation —trauma scene restoration. Point is—they're the people who come out and clean blood, bodily fluids, and other potentially dangerous materials following less than desirable situations. It's a specialty. A career path people actually chose. So many possibilities, when you think of it. So many paths one can take. I can almost hear my father saying, *your imagination is your only limitation.*

He may have been wrong about that, judging by the state of this room. The business of death cleanup requires a cold disposition and a strong stomach. And unfortunately, I have only one of the two.

What I also don't have is time.

Twenty-four minutes. The clock is running down, and I have no timeouts left. Time marches on, reminding me even the best-laid plans rarely go off without a hitch.

Hitches. Now there's something I'm familiar with. I just hadn't expected one of this magnitude. *That* was my mistake. But it wasn't the first one, and looking around, it isn't going to be the last.

I slide my phone into my back pocket again and open the closet. I could stuff them in there. Maybe. Unfortunately, old houses have small closets, and it would take quite a bit of effort to make them fit. And perhaps a few broken bones.

For a second, I think I might actually be losing it and I wonder if this is what they mean by the term *psychotic break*. I consider calling someone. *But who?* What kind of friend do you call to get you out of a jam like this?

Problem is, I know exactly what kind of friend.

But I won't go there. *I can't go there.*

Bad things happen when I go there.

Things worse than this.

You wouldn't think anything could be worse than this.

But again, you wouldn't understand.

I hope you're not offended. I'm not saying you're stupid or anything.

It's not you.

Most people wouldn't understand.

Probably not even these two, I tell myself, and then I don't know why I do it, but I lean down, pull back the covers, and really take them in. The waxy skin, the bloated faces, or what's left of them anyway, the transfixed eyes. You might think they look peaceful, but you would be wrong. This is the stuff nightmares are made of. And I see many in my future.

My phone dings. The sound startles me, and I practically leap into the bed with them. My knee bumps the mattress, and a hand flops over the side, brushing my bare skin. Every expletive I know floods my mind as I dance back. They'd come pouring out of my mouth, but I'm too afraid to open it. My phone dings again. I stare at the hand and think: *this can't be real.* Then I back away and read the text. *Where are you? I can't believe this is happening. Finally.*

He has no idea.

This is sick, he writes.

I look around the room. *Truly.*

Sick as in a BFD.

I know what you mean; I text back. He likes it when I'm up on my acronyms. He is not one who likes to explain himself, and he reads minds like it's his profession.

It is a big effing deal.

It's not every day that you hold an engagement party of this magnitude at your venue, but that is exactly what is happening in precisely twenty-one minutes. The entire town will be here. What a disaster this is going to turn out to be. Looking back, I should have said no. I tried to say no. I did say no.

It didn't work. And anyway, as for him being here, it was a favor to make up for that other favor.

My phone chimes again. *Thank God for small favors!*

I shake my head. It appears a favor is what got me into this, and a favor is going to have to be what gets me out.

CHAPTER ONE

Ruth

Then

The whimpering sound is unmistakable. It sounds like a wounded animal, only different—different in the way that you know it's human. I am casually jogging across the courthouse lawn, away from my car, making my way toward Elm Street, where the parade will start. I'm breathing hard, because I'm late and also more out of shape than I thought.

I'd sworn my phone was in my pocket until I got all the way to the main stage and realized it wasn't. Of course, this meant I had to turn around and go all the way back to the car, and now I am jogging, which is a bit of a glorification. It's actually more like speed walking, old-lady style. I am not old.

But I feel that way.

Man, do I feel that way.

Especially now that I'm doubled over, trying to suck in air. Now that I have an extreme stabbing pain in my side. Still, I am determined to make it back in time to see our float, even if that means I'm panting like a dog on a hot day when I get there. Even if it means having a heart attack at the halfway mark. Even if it means coughing up a lung on the courthouse lawn, and it feels like that is exactly what could happen any second. Sudden death seems imminent in a way that makes me question my attachment to my phone.

I would have just as soon left it, but Johnny's on call tonight, and Johnny can never be trusted to answer his phone, which means leaving mine in the car was not an option. I can't say I blame him. This thing is like a shock collar I can never get rid of. On the bright side, it has a camera, and it plays music.

That's really a long-winded way of telling you how it was I found myself near the gazebo searching for a wounded animal that was undoubtedly human, using nothing but pure instinct, and you know, the flashlight on my phone. Another positive, another feature I couldn't live without. I'm supposed to focus on the positive, or so I've been told. It's quite a long story, but don't worry we'll get there. If I don't die of a heart attack first. Which I might, because I've just spotted bare feet sticking out of a row of shrubs. Small feet. Feminine feet.

Upon closer inspection, I see a pale yellow dress shifted up, exposing more than should be exposed. *Jesus Christ.* Whatever it was I expected, it wasn't this. The girl is laying on her side, alternating between shallow sobs and serious whimpers. Another girl is hunched over her. A small crowd gathers. There are hushed whispers and worried looks. No one steps forward to help.

I kneel beside the girl, my knees sinking into the cool earth. She must sense I'm there, but she does not move. Her hair partially covers her face. Her dress is bunched up around her waist. One sandal is on her left foot, the other is I don't know where. As she cries, the scent of stale beer fills the surrounding air. It comes in waves.

"Hey," I say, leaning forward. I study the girl hunched over her, who I now realize is older than I thought, and I ask what happened.

"I don't know." Her eyes convey fear, but her voice comes out steady. She shrugs. "I found her like this."

She rests her hand on the girl's forearm, and I try to place her. I assume she's a tourist, because while she looks familiar, in the way tourists tend to do, I don't think I've ever seen her before. For sure, we've never met. You don't forget a face like that.

The girl blanches at the woman's touch. I'm not expecting it, nor is the woman. The girl rears up and then quickly shifts, cowering like a cornered animal. Her eyes are wide and glassy. She shows her teeth. She's panting harder than I am, and that's saying something. "Whoa," the woman whispers. "Easy." The woman speaks slowly as she backs away. "You're okay. See?"

I push myself up to a standing position and glance toward the parade. The girl needs a ride home, and I don't want to be the one to offer.

When I look down, she has her hands up, at first in defense, but when the woman backs off further, the girl drops one hand and uses the back of the other to wipe her face.

"You need a ride home?" the woman asks. It's the first time I notice how pretty she is.

The girl shakes her head. She can't be more than fifteen.

"Are you sure?" The woman crouches before dropping to a seated position. "I can help you get home."

The girl fingers the hem of her dress. She doesn't meet the woman's eye, but she doesn't look away either. It's obvious that a battle is raging inside her. She knows she needs help. She's too prideful—or scared—to take it.

"We've all been there," she tells the girl. "Don't worry, I won't say anything to your parents."

The girl shifts suddenly, and I shift too. My flashlight, which is still on but is pointed at the ground, shines in her direction. That's when I see the blood smeared across her thigh. Suddenly everything clicks into place. She's not just a drunken girl left behind by friends in the park.

"Who did this?" I demand, kneeling beside her. "Who left you here?"

She opens her mouth, only to close it again. Tears stream down her face. She does not meet my eye. Her gaze is far off, like it's stuck back in the past.

The woman clears her throat. "Is there someone I can call?" She glances at me as she asks, a disapproving look on her face. *Your parents* are what I'm thinking, but that's not what she says, "A friend?"

The girl looks at me. "You're Ruth, right?" Her voice shakes, but I don't think it's on account of the booze.

"Yes," I nod. "I'm Ruth."

The woman glances at me and narrows her eyes. Then she turns to the girl. "I'm Ashley."

I want to like Ashley. Mostly, because I want her to handle this situation so I don't have to. But she isn't making it easy. This isn't a goddamned pow-wow. This isn't the time for introductions. And anyway, I know the girl.

Gabby. She works at the ice cream shop on Main Street, and she shares half of her DNA with the love of my life. *Former* love of my life, I should say. Once upon a time. A lifetime ago. "And you're—"Ashley starts. She pauses and waits and when nothing comes, she waits some more.

I roll my eyes.

Finally, she runs her fingers over a patch on the girl's backpack, which is on the ground next to her. "Gabby?"

"Gabriella," the girl says, correcting her. She tries to sound grown up, authoritative even, but her voice cracks as she speaks. I think about making a run for it, but the crowd around us is growing larger. Around here people talk. Channings do not simply walk away. And anyway, I'd never forgive myself if I did. I tried that once, a long time ago. I'm not sure I have it in me anymore.

Gabby pulls at several blades of grass, ripping them from the ground one by one. She doesn't look at me as she does it. She doesn't look at Ashley either. "I know what you're thinking."

"Who did this?" I say again, because what else is there to say? White, fiery rage burns inside of me. I am definitely missing the parade. I will not see our float in all its glory. I'm going to have to call the police, which is a shame. This girl's night appears to have been bad enough, and it's about to get worse. My stomach flip-flops at the thought of what I'm about to do. My sweaty palm grips my phone, a reminder that if I hadn't forgotten it, this would be someone else's problem.

I'm aware of how that sounds. But if I know anything, I know some stories are better learned secondhand. "Gabriella," I say, leveling with her. "I need you to tell me who did this."

She chokes up at my question. Ashley gives me the death stare, which is not only annoying because it is, but because she's gorgeous even with her face all twisted up like that. The sobbing goes on for what feels like forever. Long enough for me to send several text messages. Finally, Gabby looks up and meekly, almost inaudibly, says, "I should have said no. I didn't say no."

CHAPTER TWO

Anonymous a.k.a Passerby

It's hard to stay anonymous in this day and age. Not impossible. But far from easy. It requires staying out of the fray. Or above the fray. However the saying goes.

So I guess that's where I'll start. It's important. Staying above the fray, that is.

It's important. And she's terrible at it. I really don't know why she has to go and get herself into these situations. You might have thought I was referring to that other girl, but...no. I mean, lots of girls get themselves into *those* situations. Of course, it's not their fault. No one is victim blaming or victim shaming or whatever it is they're calling it today.

Least of all me. She was a pretty girl. And it's really too bad. A lesson learned for her the hard way: You can't trust people. Not even when they say they're your friend. Sometimes, *especially* not when they say they're your friend.

Not even when they tell you they love you. Sometimes, *especially* not when they tell you they love you.

Which is kinda sorta, you could say, how I, too, found myself wrapped up in this mess.

I've hurt lots of people. I didn't hurt that girl. You can bet I have plans for who did. It's almost too easy. Considering everyone knows who it was. Small towns do not hold their secrets well.

Before you go thinking I'm some sort of hero, allow me to save you the trouble of being wrong. I'm the furthest thing from it. I won't try too hard to convince you. Believe me, time will take care of that.

CHAPTER THREE

Ruth

I was born with the cord wrapped around my neck. I guess that's where my bad luck started. Mama liked to say I was cursed. She said it like she was joking, but the older I get, the less I'm sure. She always dressed it up, usually with one of her platitudes. Mama had a lot of those. Usually, she'd add something about it making me stronger, or say that whatever ill-fated scenario was happening in my life was simply the Channing way. We are survivors, she often said, even if just barely.

This is what it feels like as I stand there waiting for the ambulance to arrive. Waiting and not wanting to see Ryan Jenkins. Or his lovely wife. Not wanting to see the agony on his face, agony that would be on any parent's face.

Not wanting to remember.

This is also what it feels like the first time I meet Ashley Parker. Having a cord wrapped around my neck. Suffice it to say, Davis's latest girlfriend is not my cup of tea. First the police arrive, and by police I mean Roy. He calls in a female officer, as is protocol. I would have texted her, too, at the start, but she's new in town and so far, we're not on a first-name basis. I was hoping that wouldn't change. Although, knowing Roy, of course it would.

But then, I'm getting ahead of myself.

Every Channing baby for generations back was thrust in the world that same way. With our cords around our necks. Lots of Channings died before they'd ever gotten a start. There's a whole cemetery filled with baby Channings, somewhere west of town. I never go there, but Mama did.

Only Davis had been different. He didn't come into the world like the rest of us. It was almost like he was the chosen one or something, which Mama always thought he was.

She wanted more children and would've had them had it not been on account of the babies in the cemetery. I don't know when it got to be too much for her, because when you're a kid, there's a lot of stuff you don't know. But at some point it did, and that's how even though Daddy always said he wanted a whole zoo full of kids, or a slew of them, which sounded to me at the time like he was saying a *zoo*, it ended up being just Johnny and Davis and me.

That's not to say we were alone. We had—we *have*—tons of cousins. No one ever leaves Jester Falls.

No one but Davis.

His unconventional and ill-timed idea planted the seed that would be the ultimate manifestation of me meeting Ashley Parker face to face, here and now. Some things, they start small, and they grow and they grow and they grow. I know that. But I don't think I *knew* it. There's a difference. And as it turns out, it's quite a big one.

One morning, out of the blue, Davis waltzed into the kitchen and, over Julia's famous biscuits and gravy, announced that he was going on a cross-country trip. The nerve. Upsetting Julia that way. And the way he said it, like it was nothing. Like leaving Magnolia House to Johnny and me to take care of was no big deal. He dressed it up, kind of like Mama used to do with her platitudes. He said he wanted to see how other bed and breakfasts were staying afloat in the age of Airbnb and all the rental sites and whatnot. Funny thing is, Jester Falls is a tight-knit community. You could call it exclusive, if you want. That would be putting it politely. Which is why I never believed Davis. We don't have the kind of people here who want to rent out their homes. What happens between our walls tends to stay there.

I know because...well, let's just say I know. The real estate developers have been coming to town with their fancy ideas and dollar signs in their eyes for as long as I can remember. Jester Falls is the type of town where they're run right back out, with their tails tucked between their legs.

As for Davis, I wasn't sure what he was going after. Greener pastures, maybe, and in a sense, looking at Ms. America here, I guess that's what he found.

———

DAVIS CALLED ME FROM THE ROAD EXACTLY TWO DAYS AGO. HE should have sounded happy. He should have sounded free, but he didn't. Anyone else in that position, they would've sounded happy. Anyone else who managed to escape the back-breaking labor of the hospitality industry, anyone else who'd shirked their family responsibility, would have sounded elated.

But he didn't. He sounded pensive and worried. And perhaps a little restless.

"I picked up a woman," he announced.

"What, like a hooker?" His voice sounded funny, like he was whispering, like he was trying not to be heard. So I didn't know what he meant. I didn't know what the big secret was. I didn't expect him to say what he said.

"Like a hitchhiker."

My brother is maybe a little naïve. But he isn't stupid.

Although Johnny would argue with that. I might too, if we were in the same room together. For posterity's sake, Davis is wicked smart. Earned himself a full ride and passed the bar exam on the first try. He barely even studied.

"A hitchhiker?" This was exactly something my little brother would do, and still I had to ask. "Why would you do that?"

"I don't know." He sounded far away. "Anyway, she's sort of sick. I think we're going to lie low for a few days."

"Lie low? Where are you?"

"New Orleans."

"Louisiana? Why?"

"It's a long story."

"Clearly."

I waited for him to say more, but he didn't. So naturally, I filled the silence. "Davis?"

"Yeah?"

"I have time." It was a lie. We'd been booked solid for weeks, with no chance of things slowing soon. Not with the summer season upon us.

"I know."

"You're not in trouble, are you?"

"No, it's nothing like that."

"You'd tell me if you were?"

"Of course."

I wanted to believe him. At one point I would have. This time I didn't.

"She's not underage, is she?"

"Jesus, Ruth. No."

"You sound nervous. Why do you sound nervous?"

"The reason I'm calling, actually... is—" His voice cut out. It was several seconds before I could hear him again. "I wanted to know if you could get the place cleaned up?"

"Hmm?"

"The house."

"What house?" I knew what he was saying and suddenly everything made sense, and yet it didn't.

"Magnolia House." The phone jostled and then he came back, his voice clearer. "Can you hear me okay?"

"I can hear you fine."

"Good. Anyway...like I said—we're going to lie low here for a few days. Just until she's feeling better." There was a rustling noise in the background, and the line went quiet for a second.

"Davis?"

"Yeah—sorry. I think it's just dehydration. It's really humid here."

"So you're coming home?"

"The beach and the fresh air will do her good."

"So you'll be home in time for the Watermelon Festival, then?"

"I think so."

"It's in two days."

"I know when it is, Ruth." He exhaled deeply, right into the speaker. Right into my ear. Purposely and righteously. The way Daddy used to. It shouldn't have, but it made me miss them both. "I've been there every year of my life."

"Great," I quipped. "Then you won't end your streak."

"I didn't plan this."

I didn't know what he meant by that. And I didn't ask. I had a million other questions floating through my mind. None of them seemed to want to be asked. I just wanted him home. I hadn't wanted him to leave in the first place. "Are you sure you're okay? You don't sound okay."

His voice hardened. Davis didn't get angry often. But he had his limits and once you'd crossed them, he had a way of letting you know. "I said I'm fine." He sighed heavily. "Good bye, Ruth. I'll call you when I'm on the road."

Davis left me hanging, so I did the opposite of what I should have done, which was to keep my mouth shut, and I went to find

Johnny. I spilled the tea, and I did it in a big way. The Channing way.

"You need to mind your own business," Johnny said.

"He made it my business!"

"And now, what? You're making it mine?"

"I just thought you should know."

"That's just it, though, Ruth. There's nothing to know! You're just making things up—out of thin air!"

"He called, Johnny. Davis called me. Why didn't he just show up? Why didn't he just come home? It felt like a warning. Like he might have gotten himself in some sort of trouble." I swallowed hard. "He sounded like he was in trouble."

"Well, he didn't call *me*."

"So, what?" I threw my hands up. "You don't care?"

He looked at me for a long time before he spoke. "Frankly, no. No, I don't. And you shouldn't either. Davis is—well, you know how he is. Same as he's always been." He ran his hand along the length of his jaw. "Things will play out the way they're supposed to. And there's nothing you can do about it."

"Sure there is."

"Whatever is going on with Davis—if anything—it doesn't concern you, Ruth. Let it be." He crossed the room, and I thought the conversation would end there. I almost wish it would have. "You can't fix other people's problems. And anyway, you have enough of your own."

"This isn't just anyone! This is our brother."

Johnny put his hands on his hips and lowered his gaze to the floor. "I don't know what to tell you," he said, shaking his head. He took several long breaths before looking up again. "You never learn."

A part of me knew Davis hadn't called because he wanted to know if I could get the place cleaned up, or because in two days' time, they'd be back here in Jester Falls. He couldn't have meant that. If there's one thing Mama taught us, it was the meaning of clean.

After I relayed the conversation to Johnny, I was annoyed that he didn't provide the answers I was hoping for. Instead, he took personal offense to it. I guess I should have known. Johnny takes offense to everything.

CHAPTER FOUR

Ruth

"What kind of monster would do something like this?" Johnny asks as he paces back and forth. He looks so much like Daddy—he always has. But even more so standing here tonight. Maybe it's the concern etched on his face. Maybe it's the volunteer fire department T-shirt, or the way he carries himself, with his hands on his hips, his shoulders slightly slouched. He's a mountain of a man. He towers over me. He towers over most people.

"No, seriously," he says, repeating himself. "What kind of fucking monster would do this?"

"The kind that gets handled," Cole says. We're all just standing there, among the crowd which has gathered and is growing in size, watching Roy and the female officer and the paramedics do their jobs. It feels like nothing is happening and everything is happening, which can often sum up life in this town.

"Not now," I say to Cole, looking over at Ashley and back at him. "This isn't the time."

Cole's gaze flits from Ashley to me and then to Johnny. His eyes ask the question that's on everyone's mind. Everyone but mine. And hers. What is it about men, always being the last to know? Cole is asking in his way who she is and if she's with Johnny, although I can tell he assumes. I can also tell Johnny is wondering the exact same thing. He has no idea who she is. But he wants to.

Cole leans toward Ashley and extends his hand. I watch as she takes it, expecting to feel nothing, and I almost succeed.

"I'm Ashley," she smiles. "Ashley Parker." I roll my eyes because finally Cole has met someone who is as well-mannered as he is.

Cole is Johnny's best friend. Has been since they were toddlers. Why is anyone's guess. The two of them couldn't be any more different. That, and, Johnny never has been very good at keeping friends. Davis likes to say that if it weren't for me, Cole would've been long gone by now. Knowing him, though, that's not true. There are good dogs less loyal than Cole Wheeler.

Johnny looks at me. My brows raise. He nods a hello at Ashley. It's clear what he thinks of our little brother's latest love interest. She might as well be a ghost.

"When did you guys get in?" I say to Ashley. Partly because I'm curious, partly because I hadn't expected to meet like this.

"Just a few hours ago."

We all watch as they load the girl onto the stretcher. They've barely closed the ambulance doors when her parents pull up and the crowd parts to give them room to move through. Cole watches me closely. I pretend not to notice.

"Where's Davis?" Johnny asks. He's looking at Ashley as he says it, but he's speaking to all of us.

"He's driving the Thompsons' float," Cole says.

"He had to run back to the house," I say at the same time.

"He said there was something he had to handle," Ashley says.

The words spill out in the way that makes it obvious she wishes she could take them back.

"Well, which is it?" Johnny demands.

We all stand there, surrounded by flashing lights, shrugging in unison.

DAVIS ISN'T THE TYPE NOT TO SHOW UP FOR THE PARADE. HE ISN'T the type to just leave his date on the courthouse lawn, so I know something is wrong. I know there is something Ashley Parker isn't saying, and I am pretty sure I know what that something is.

I just hope I'm wrong.

Ashley rubs her temples and then rolls her neck. Suddenly, she takes hold of Cole's forearm. "I'm sorry," she says. "I'm feeling a little dizzy."

Cole's expression goes from confused to reluctant to ready to help in nanoseconds. I don't miss any of it. "Here," he tells her, taking her by the elbow. "Sit down."

"Can you call Davis?" she asks shakily. "I think I need to go back to the house and lie down."

"I've tried," Johnny huffs. He motions at me. "Ruth, drive her to the house." He doesn't tell me he'll find Davis when he orders me around, but it's clear that's what he means.

"I'll do it," Cole says with a sigh. It's slight, that sigh, but it's there. I know in the way he is looking at me. He knows I don't want to drive her home. He sees the concern in my eyes. Cole can see straight through me. And I hate every second of it.

I don't thank him, even though I should. He'd do anything for me. Still, I know this is no small favor.

"I hate to miss the parade," Ashley says, holding her head in her hands. She's got the damsel in distress down pat, that's for sure. I blink hard several times. No one notices. It's hard to believe this is a grown woman I'm hearing and seeing. I want to feel sorry for her, but I just can't muster the energy.

That doesn't stop Cole or Johnny from doing it. While my brother is stoic in his usual way, I can see he sees Ashley Parker for what she is. A liability. And a fragile one.

"It's sort of a big deal," Cole says, helping her to her feet. He looks over at me. "But don't worry. There's always next year."

CHAPTER FIVE

Ruth

Cole is right about one thing. The annual parade is a big deal. Floats have been worked on for months, tractor trailers have been all decorated up, businesses around town have given it their all while they have the eyes of the entire town. Not just our town, but the eyes of the tourists who've descended in order to take their picturesque shots for social media, make their cotton candy memories, and hopefully after a brief stay at Magnolia House, leave just the way they came.

Aside from the parade, kick-off night is when the Watermelon Queen is announced. All the contestants line up, smile nervously, and wave from the stage, wearing evening gowns they've fretted over for months. It's not exactly what you'd call a feminist-friendly occasion, as has been written on many a travel blogs, considering the pageantry of it all. But Jester Falls is steeped in tradition, and this one would have to be pried from our cold, dead hands.

I was crowned Watermelon Queen once, a decade ago. Although, those days have faded into memories I no longer care to relive. Except, sometimes I do relive them. Especially on nights like this, especially when I am haunted by thoughts of him. As soon as I find Davis, I know how the rest of this night will go. I'll do what I always do. I'll put on an old record, pour a glass of brandy and go through Mama's photo albums. The covers are worn, the pages so well picked through that I worry they won't hold up. But each time they somehow do and I wonder why no one makes albums anymore, why everything has to be digital and fleeting. There's something about the tactile feeling of holding a physical reminder in your hands that makes it feel important. That makes it feel real. Mama used to say history is what keeps you from forgetting where you came from.

I'm not sure she knew how many people actually want to forget.

If only it were that simple. I'm thinking about her in that cemetery when two teenagers knock me from behind. I turn to find them giggling, dressed in evening gowns, trying to snap a selfie. They do not apologize—in fact, if they see me standing there, they don't acknowledge it.

"Excuse me," one of them says, and I am thankful to be wrong. She holds out her phone. "Would you mind taking a picture of us?"

I take it from her and consider snapping several photos of myself instead and handing it back. But I've recently set a new goal to only reach for pettiness in extreme situations, and also, I notice the Watermelon Queen sash around her. I remember being that age. Barely.

I position the phone, snap a photo, and hand it back to her. She glances at the screen, brings it close to her face, studies it, and scrunches her nose. Then she shows her friend, shakes her head and thrusts the phone in my direction. "Would you mind taking another?"

Actually, I would. But that's not what I say. I take several shots, hand the phone back, wait for the approval of a teenager, and think about how far I've let myself go. Finally, she looks up at me and shrugs. "I guess it'll do."

Her friend says, "We can filter it."

No one says thank you.

I stand there, annoyed, and I search the crowd, thinking about the past, thinking how much better it must have been when everyone didn't try so hard. When everything didn't feel so manufactured, when people didn't have to make their memories perfect, with exactly the right shot—and maybe that's the problem. Now people expect things will live forever. It used to be that someone could write something bad about your town, or your place of business, and it would be gone the next day. Now, it lives in digital form forever, only to be repurposed and shared in controversial bits, bits that never quite tell the whole story. There's a lot that can happen between perfect takes. I could've strangled the Watermelon Queen, for example. I certainly pictured it in my mind.

My eyes aren't the only thing scanning the crowd. I pick up bits and pieces of conversation, mostly small town gossip, but also threads about what happened with the girl we found by the courthouse. I listen to two women talking: Georgia, who runs the floral shop, and Anita Bealls, who was widowed last year and owns a boutique but spends all her time shopping. You have to be careful about making eye contact with her. Any conversation vacillates between her ocean of grief and her latest internet find.

But now she's onto a different topic, which doesn't happen often. Which is probably why I listen. "All I'm saying is you ought to be prepared. When word gets out, the tourists will stop coming. I can't say I'd blame them. It's not safe."

Georgia waves her off. "It's terrible. But unfortunately these things happen."

Anita's hand flies to her chest. "Not in Jester Falls, they don't."

Georgia furrows her brow. She wants to argue but rape is a tricky subject to navigate. "I'll be praying for the Jenkins tomorrow in church. I'm sure we all will."

"I don't know," Anita says. "I hear even church attendance has dropped." She shakes her head slowly from side to side, clutching her actual pearls. "This town is changing. It's not the same as it was when I moved here. Back when Bill and I were married."

Georgia takes offense, but she does it the way most women in this town do, politely with a bit of an edge. "Well," she answers with a smile. She places her hand on Anita's forearm. "I was born here. And summer season at First Baptist has always ebbed and flowed. Everything will be fine. There's no need to worry. And like my mama said..." She leans in close and lowers her chin, leveling her eyes. "Worrying gives you wrinkles."

"Maybe," Anita quips. "But I just hope word doesn't get out that we have a rapist on the loose, or I'm going to be buying a lot more flowers to save your ass."

I can't help but laugh, even though nothing is really funny, considering, but I can't stop. I laugh until tears well in my eyes, until eventually the two women turn and look at me. Anita looks me over from head to toe while Georgia Adkins goes about it a little more subtly.

"I guess she's been drinking again," Anita says, turning her back to me.

Georgia follows suit. "It's a shame. She's so pretty. Always has been. You should have seen her when she was little. She turned heads on the street, that girl. People stopped to watch her go by. Now, it's almost like she's stopped trying."

"That's what happens when girls don't listen. They think they can have it all. And then they become old maids."

"Who drink too much." She ribs Anita. "What's your excuse, then?"

"I'm a widow. And I'm already old," Anita laughs. "But yeah, I mean, who can blame her?"

"Did you catch the Johnsons' float?" Georgia asks. "I thought they did a lovely job. We supplied the flowers, but they did all the work."

"The who?" Anita cocks her head. "Oh and hey— about the Channing girl." She points in my direction. "Look at her. I really do think something's wrong with her."

"Ruth is Ruth," Georgia says. She and I do a fair amount of business together. Surely she knows I can hear them.

"No," Anita says, "It's that entire family. I've always thought there was something off about them. Bill always thought so, too."

I WALK TOWARD THE CARNIVAL WITH MY PHONE PRESSED TO MY EAR. The scent of popcorn and nostalgia fill the air. I listen to my voicemail, two of which are from Julia, and one is about a reservation.

I try Davis again, and when it goes to voicemail, I send a text. I consider going back to the house. There's no point in being here.

And anyway, I know that photo albums, old records, and brandy await me at home. It's like they're reaching out, beckoning me, proving to me where I belong. All the elements are in place for that kind of disaster. Those women, the situation at the courthouse, seeing Ryan, reminiscing about the past. Thinking of what could have been. Thinking how much can change in an instant. Thinking he knows that now. He's living it.

I glance back at the stage, where a slideshow is playing. Photos flash across the screen displaying all the former Watermelon Queens. Mama's photo is there, but I know I won't stay long enough to see it.

I think about what Jester Falls must have been like then, and I wonder if Anita is right. Maybe things have changed and not for the better. Surely they faced controversies too. But I have a hard time coming up with anything significant, even though I know this can't be true. Things are never as perfect as they seem.

Finally, I spot Johnny near the food stands chatting up a group of Rotary Club members, men twice his age. That's Johnny for you. He always has his hand in some sort of pot, and he's always stirring. He gives me a look, which is to say he hasn't found Davis, as though it isn't obvious, so I text Cole.

Johnny didn't find Davis. Can you check the Holts' place?

He replies within seconds. *Already did.*

I ask myself why Davis would have gone there, but it's a pointless question, one I already know the answer to. My little brother has to play the hero. He always has.

I just hope I'm wrong.

My phone vibrates in my hand. I pray it's Davis but Cole's name lights up the screen. *Don't worry. I'll find him.*

I scan the crowd, and my eyes land on Johnny, who hasn't moved. He flashes an irritated look in my direction, the kind that makes me wish Davis would get his shit together. That way the rest of us wouldn't have to be out here propping the world up with our own two hands.

CHAPTER SIX

Ruth

Cole didn't find Davis at the Holts' place because he'd already been there and gone. He wasn't at the parade, and he wasn't at home, because he was in the emergency room. It sounds bad, and it is, but not for the reasons you think. Davis is pretty lucky that he isn't in jail or worse—dead.

Cole calls the ER and then me when he finds him, and even though I'm stone-cold sober, I ask Johnny to drive me to the hospital. Because if there's one thing Davis is going to need, aside from medical attention, it's the protection of his big brother.

I don't know what he was thinking. It's a sentiment I've held where he is concerned far too frequently lately. Davis should have known better. Everyone knows you do not mess with a Holt and get away with it. The same way you don't mess with a Channing. The difference is the Holts will kill you in broad daylight and not think twice about it, whereas we Channings like to go about things in a slightly more civilized manner.

"What the fuck were you thinking?" I say the second the emergency room attendant opens the door to the small exam room. It smells like antiseptic and bad decisions, and the combination fills me with rage. "And you drove yourself here? In this condition?"

The attendant looks from me to my little brother, wearing a blank stare and a sly smirk. It's obvious that not only does she see a lot in her occupation, but she enjoys it.

"What are you looking at?" I step forward, straightening my spine. She doesn't flinch, she doesn't bat an eye—not until Johnny steps in, anyway.

He offers his signature grin, dimples and all. That grin has an effect on women that I'll never understand. Most women in this town say it's the dark hair and the even darker eyes, that or the tan skin and broad shoulders. But probably it's the grin. Either way, it's disgusting. Although, it did earn me a number of friends in high school and college that I wouldn't have otherwise had.

"You'll have to forgive my sister." He motions with his hands as though he's knocking a few drinks back. "She has a hard time understanding her limit."

The girl is putty in his hands. All smiles and head tilts. She nods at Davis lying on the gurney. "Looks like it runs in the family."

Johnny towers over her. He leans in like a Cheshire cat, eyeing its prey. I scan the room for the vomit bin. He clears his throat and then lowers his voice. "You have no idea."

Thankfully, there's a knock at the door which saves us all from me losing my lunch, both physically and metaphorically. "Well, well," a booming voice says, stepping into the small room. "What have we here?"

I'd know that voice anywhere. "Ruth?"

I smile at Dr. Erichs, Jester Fall's oldest veterinarian, as he pushes the curtain back.

"I guess I should ask the same," Davis coughs out. It's clear he's in pain and not simply because there's a gash in his forehead or blood all over his shirt. It's not just the black eye or the ice pack covering his right hand. It's in his voice. My little brother's voice gives everything away, always. It's his biggest tell.

"Well, my boy, this is what happens when you live in a small town and the only other doctor on emergency call is dealing with a kid with a concussion and another waiting with a broken arm. You get me."

Davis shifts. "Is that even legal?"

"The Good Samaritan Law, look it up," Dr. Erichs says. "Unless, of course, you'd rather wait around all night..."

"No," Davis answers with a wince. "I just hope you brought the good drugs."

"I take it you were feeling a bit tougher a few hours ago," Dr. Erichs remarks. It makes me think of the two summers I spent interning with him, back when I thought I'd trade the hospitality business for the animal one, back before I realized they're all the same beast.

It was a hard lesson to learn, but not the hardest. If only I'd known at the time, I'm sure I would have spent less time feeling miserable about it. Daddy had been furious at me over the situation. It was one of the few things I ever heard him and Mama truly argue about. *You have to let her learn,* Mama had said. *She'll come to her senses.*

Mama was right.

There was no way I was getting away from Magnolia House. Perhaps in a different life. I learned in those two summers that the things you love, you also come to hate, but you have to choose your battles. Also, Daddy usually got what he wanted, and this case was no different.

Johnny reaches out to shake Dr. Erichs hand, and then with a nod he slumps down in one of two plastic chairs.

"I'm sorry you had to come out so late," I say.

He waves me off. "It's par for the course. Carnivals and bouncy houses—" He stops mid-sentence as he pulls back the makeshift bandage on Davis's forehead. "They're good for business."

"I still want to know what you were thinking," I say, gripping the handrails of the gurney.

"You're going to need some sutures in that hand, too," Dr. Erichs says, looking him over.

So while Davis is getting his hand sewn up, I keep asking him what in the fuck he was thinking and he keeps deflecting by asking where Ashley is.

Finally, I say, "Cole took her home."

"Are you sure? She isn't answering her cell or the house phone."

"Why would she? She doesn't live there."

I know what my brother is thinking. He's thinking he doesn't trust the Holts. He's thinking about retaliation. But it isn't Magnolia House at the forefront of his mind, and it really should be.

"They're going to kill you," I say, and Johnny waves me off.

"No one is going to kill anyone."

"Sure they are. They'll kill him."

Dr. Erichs gets a call. I watch closely as he deftly silences his phone with one hand while threading sutures with the other. "I wouldn't worry too much, Ruth. That family's more bark than bite."

I can tell he's lying because I know Dr. Erichs. Working with large animals requires a certain kind of trust. You learn to read cues real quick. And he taught me well.

His phone rings again. "I'm sorry," he says. "I need to take this."

We can't help but listen to the muffled voice coming from his phone as a woman speaks in a hurried tone. Dr. Erichs responds with a series of questions. It doesn't sound good.

He ends the call and points at the sutures. He tells us he has to go and then he hands me the scissors. "You okay to take over, Ruth?"

At first I think he is kidding, but then I remember Dr. Erichs doesn't kid. I motion toward my brother. "What about Johnny? He's the EMT."

"I'm off duty," Johnny says, which is a lie. He's never really off duty.

I don't want to seem petty in front of Dr. Erichs, so I shrug. "Sure, I'll fix his face."

When I walk over to the sink to scrub my hands, Davis closes his eyes and lets out a long and heavy sigh. "This better get me a discount on my bill."

"You should have waited," Johnny says to Davis after Dr. Erichs leaves the room. "Why didn't you wait?"

"He knocked Ashley to the ground and then he ran off. What was I supposed to do, let him go?"

"Yes," Johnny and I shout at the same time.

"After what he did to that girl?" He moves as he speaks, and I almost drop the needle. "You two think I should just let him get away with it?"

"That's what cops are for," Johnny says. He doesn't mean it, at least not when it comes to personal matters, but I appreciate the effort.

"The Holts get away with enough, don't you think?"

"With worse," Johnny says. "Yes."

"What's worse than what he did to her?"

Johnny shakes his head. "Let's hope you don't find out."

"We don't know it was Bobby Holt," I say.

"The hell we don't. Everyone in this town knows it was him. And this is what—the third time something like this has happened?"

"Still." I pull the last stitch through and tie it off. "You shouldn't have gone after him alone."

"I did okay."

I tap the ice pack on his hand, causing him to wince. "You sure about that?"

Johnny clears his throat. "How'd you come to be involved?"

"I saw Kurt Latham across the street, and I jogged over to ask how the boat repair was coming."

My brow raises. "He's had it forever."

"You know how Kurt is…"

Johnny cocks his head. "And?"

"Ashley was waiting for me across the street. By the court-house. Said she wanted to read the plaque near the gazebo, and that's when she stumbled on the situation…"

"So she saw Bobby Holt attacking the girl?"

His eyes narrow. "No, but he was near her. And she was crying."

"And then what?" I say.

"I helped Ashley to her feet and checked her over and then I followed him. I hopped into my truck and followed him straight to his house."

"Did you kill him?" Johnny asks.

"No. But he won't be messing with any girls anytime soon. Let's put it that way."

Johnny rubs his jaw. "You should have killed him."

"I don't want to go to prison."

"Yeah, well, what you have instead is a permanent target on your back."

I don't say it. But I don't disagree.

CHAPTER SEVEN

Ruth

I don't see Ashley Parker again until the following morning. I'm in the big house, known to guests as Magnolia House, but home to me, when I hear the screen door at the front of the house creak open and then slam shut.

I stare out the window over the kitchen sink, looking out into the garden. It feels like someone is watching me. Little hairs at the base of my neck stand on end, as though there's an electric energy around, the kind that can be felt but not seen.

Outside, everything seems fine. Inside may be a different story, but out there, the sun is shining and the birds are chirping. I can't deny it's a beautiful morning, even if I've hardly slept and I'm hungover. Even if the events of last night are weighing heavy on my mind. Even if it feels like someone is watching me, waiting for...well, I don't know what.

I'm aggressively scrubbing at a stain on my favorite coffee mug when I hear someone come in and slide a kitchen chair across the hardwood floor. I know it's her without turning around. I can smell the fresh lilac scent of her shampoo. It smells like the rest of her looked last night on the courthouse lawn—expensive. My stomach flip-flops, the nausea building like tall waves that threaten to take me down. I felt like a drink last night after we got home from the emergency room. But then, one turned into two, which turned into I'm not sure how many.

"Good morning," she says, and even though I know she is there, even though I heard her come in and I am expecting it, I still flinch. She bids me a good morning like she means it. But I hear the disparity. There's a softness to her voice that so neatly contains its rough edges.

After I've placed the coffee mug back in its rightful spot in the cupboard, I turn to face her, resting the small of my back against the counter. It aches like the rest of me. "Morning."

A lump forms in my throat, almost against my will. She looks out of place in this kitchen, at our table. I can't recall the last time we had a guest in this part of the house. It's reserved for family and, on occasion, staff. Julia, too, of course. She is practically family.

Ashley Parker tilts her head and studies me with concern. "Everything okay?" She doesn't tell me I look like shit, but she doesn't have to. Her expression does it for her.

"Perfectly fine," I manage to reply when what I want to offer is the truth. She shouldn't be here. We don't just let anyone in. Some parts of Magnolia House are just for family. And whatever she is, she's not that.

Instead, what comes out sounds like "Coffee" with a quirked brow and a question mark on the end. Mama taught me nothing if not to be polite.

It's too warm out already to feel in the mood for hot coffee, but I woke up groggy and I wanted the comfort of the heat, so I put on a pot.

"I'd love some," she says, rising to her feet. She motions toward the coffeepot. "But I can get it. Just point me toward the cups."

She's already made her way to the cabinet, already reaching for the mug before I manage to stretch words from my brain to my mouth. I hold my breath as her fingers brush the mug I've just replaced. Daddy's mug. She takes it and sets it on the counter like it's nothing.

"Not this one," I say, snatching it off the counter, placing it back where it belongs. I pull another mug and hold it out to her. "These are for guests."

She gives me the onceover and moves in to take it. Her face remains neutral, and I hate her a bit for that. "You know what?" I pull my hand back and walk over to the coffeepot. "Here," I say, filling the cup. "Let me."

She sits slowly, smoothing her dress out, crossing her legs at the ankle. She's going to fit right in around here, and I hate her for that, too.

A gust of wind blows through the curtains, sending them flying forward, and I'm thankful for the chance to look away. From the corner of my eye, I watch as she stares out at the street. Tourists are already riding bikes, many in search of breakfast, and the early birds have already begun lugging their things down to the beach. "I don't remember it being this lovely."

I set the coffee in front of her. "Careful, it's hot."

As she wraps her hands around the cup, I take the opportunity to really look at her. She can't be a day over twenty-five, at least a full decade younger than Davis, who is a few years behind me. Her platinum blonde hair is swept up into a loose chignon, and her face is mostly perfect and bare, save for a touch of light eyeliner on her lids. A hint of mascara accentuates her pale blue eyes. She looks flawless, which isn't that hard when you're twenty-five, and I wonder what time she got up to look this put together, or if she always wakes up this way.

"You must get up early," she remarks. "In order to manage all of this."

"Usually, yes." I don't know what to say or how to move, not even in my own home. I am not one for small talk, and her eyes make me feel like a housefly that has just been pinned to a wall. Sometimes I don't sleep at all, but I don't tell her this. With fourteen guest rooms, complimentary breakfast, a wine cellar, a library and full-service concierge, there's always something to do.

"I can't imagine how you do it. Davey has only told me bits here and there—" She presses her lips to her mug. "But I get the sense it takes a lot to run this place. It's so elegant."

"It's old."

"Stunning is what it is. They don't make houses like this anymore." She reaches for the newspaper and slides it from one side of the table to the other. "And I have to say...I'm kind of surprised. In a good way. Davey didn't tell me you were this pretty."

You should have seen me a few years ago. "Speaking of—how is my brother this morning?"

She sucks in a deep breath and forces it out. "He's pretty sore. At least he's up. You know him—nothing keeps him down for long."

But do you know him? I start to ask her this, and a million other things, but then I think better of it. "And you, are you feeling better?"

"Oh, much." She folds forward, resting her elbows on the table. "I slept like a baby."

There's a thumping sound above our heads, and then a bigger racket. It sounds like someone dragging a heavy chair across the floor.

"I think Davey was right. I just needed to be near the ocean. I mean...yeah, the guest house is old, and the walls are paper thin, but I love the vibe. It's *soooo* cozy... I may never leave."

"You've visited Jester Falls before?"

"Me?" Her left hand touches her chest. "No."

"Huh." I shift from one foot to the other. "I thought you just said you didn't remember it being this lovely."

"Ah," she quips. "Well...yes...I mean...once." She sighs wistfully. "A long time ago."

I don't ask for details because I really don't care. The only thing that concerns me at the moment is what I need to do to get rid of her. "What do you do?"

"I'm sorry?"

I know she heard me and I don't think she's that dense. "For a living?"

"Oh." She smiles. "I'm a teacher..." Her smile expands to fill her entire face. "Kindergarten. I love that age."

Of course. I've never seen a teacher in my whole life that looks like her. A model, or influencer, or whatever they're calling them these days, sure. A trust fund baby, absolutely. But not a teacher.

"Interesting. Davis has told me nothing," I say, and I wonder if he even thought to ask. With looks like hers, I'm guessing not many people do.

She waves a perfectly manicured hand in the air. "Sounds like Davey. You know how men are, always leaving out the finer details."

Hearing her call him Davey sets my shoulders straight. No one has called him that, not since Mama. I wonder if she knows this. I wonder what else he's told her.

"I mean, he hasn't told me much," she offers, and she's a mind reader, this one. "He was just so excited to show me around his hometown that I couldn't help but be excited, too. And then to come in on the biggest weekend of the year, I just feel like it was meant to be, him bringing me here."

"Has it changed since the last time?" I'm fishing and she senses that.

"I really can't say." She shrugs coyly. "I was a child. I hardly remember."

You're still a child.

"I was bummed to miss the kick-off last night."

Liar.

"Sometimes I get carsick and well, the whole thing with Gabby… It was a lot," she says, and it looks like she might choke up. She's not a teacher. She's an actress.

"After Cole brought me back to the guest house—and he was so sweet, by the way, making sure I got in safe and made it into bed—I don't know what got into me, only that I was so tired, I couldn't keep my eyes open. And then, the next thing I know I woke up and Davey—"

I don't want to hear anymore, so I cut her off. I hate that she calls him that. "You have to be careful about the heat. It can really getcha if you're not used to it."

"Yeah…" She finishes her coffee. "It was just so sweet the way he tiptoed in. And then he climbed into bed and I saw his face and I couldn't believe it. The way he talked… I thought Jester Falls was safe."

"It's not safe," I lie. Or maybe this is the truth. At this point, I can't say.

"Well, someone really needs to do something about that."

"Seems like they did."

"No," she quips. "That maniac is still out there. And after what he did to Davey… Well, someone really ought to take care of him…"

"Who'd you have in mind?" I ask facetiously.

She narrows her eyes. "I'm not as naïve as I look."

Ashley Parker doesn't expand on her sentiment, and I don't ask her to. This might have been a mistake. "That," I tell her, "I'm certain of."

"Poor Davey." I wince every time she speaks. Her tone is whiny, like nails on a chalkboard, and the hangover doesn't help. "I really feel for him. He's going to be moving slow for a while."

I ignore her in favor of putting dishes away. I hired someone new last week, and no matter how many times I, or Julia, show her, she continues to do things her own way.

"He was supposed to take me dancing tonight," she sighs. "Still. I'm so proud. He's such a hero!"

"I'm not sure that's a good thing."

"Really?" Ashley cocks her head to one side and watches me closely. "Well, I slept soundly knowing."

I narrow my eyes. "Davis said he found you on the road…"

"That's right." She brushes a crumb off the table and into her hand. "God, I was so lucky he was passing by."

"Seems risky letting a stranger pick you up."

"Believe me, it was." I'm not expecting her to say anything else, but when she opens her mouth, words come pouring out. She speaks a million miles a minute. "It was stupid, really. I should have known better than to try to get anywhere in that clunker. I actually thought Davey could get me back on the road."

She watches as I wipe down the table. When I look over at her, she's shaking her head as though she's lost in thought. "In a sense, I guess he did. And now, here I am."

I offer a tight smile. It's the best I can do. "And now, here you are."

CHAPTER EIGHT

Ruth

I'm on my way to Hillford to pick up several items I have on order at the hardware store. I also need to grab a few groceries and drop by the post office.

I've shifted the car into reverse when I hear a loud thump come from the trunk. It catches me off guard, and my heart leaps into my throat. My breathing becomes taxing, as though my lungs are relearning how to function for the first time.

When I glance in the rearview mirror, I am expecting the worst, but all I see is a pretty blonde in a yellow summer dress. *Shit.* My mouth goes dry, and I get a funny feeling in my stomach. I almost wish it were one of the thousand other things my mind darted to. Anything but this. Anything but her. I pump the brakes, purposefully flashing the tail lights several times. I expect that she'll move to the side and let me pass, but she doesn't, or at least not enough to allow for a quick getaway without mowing her over.

It could solve a lot of problems, to be sure, but it would be a weak move, and I have a low-key agenda in mind for the rest of the day.

She shakily makes her way around the side of the car, high heels and uneven gravel ensuring the journey is a tricky one. She motions for me to lower my window and because I know what is coming, I am tempted to step on the gas and hightail it out of here, but then there's a strange feeling that stops me. *What if something has happened to Davis? What if, Ruth, you could somehow use this experience to your advantage?*

I don't know where these thoughts come from, only that they bother me enough to take notice.

She's all smiles, her perfectly capped teeth blinding me like the sun. "Davey said you were going into town. Mind if I tag along?"

"Yes, actually." I don't have a lot going on at the moment, but she doesn't know that. And I am certainly not going to sit around chauffeuring twenty-somethings. That's my brother's job. He brought her here. He can handle the babysitting.

Her expression falls. "Please? I promise not to be any trouble." She looks away toward the guest house, and then back at me. "I just need to run into the drugstore and grab a few things."

"I'm sorry. I'm not going by the drugstore. I'm going to the post office and the hardware store and I'm in a hurry. Maybe my brother can drive you. Either of them…"

"The post office? Oh, good. I need to pick up some stamps for the postcards I bought to send to my student."

"I can grab them for you. How many do you need?"

She grips a hold of my door like her life depends on it. "Ruth. Please."

"I—"

"Davis's truck is a stick shift. He's not feeling well, and I don't want to bother Johnny. And you're already going—"

"Fine," I hiss. "Get in."

We drive to Hillford, which is a good half-hour away, and

Ashley is mostly quiet except for the fact that she hums to the tune of every song on the radio, no matter how many times I change the station. She knows all the songs, even the classical ones without words. So eventually, I am forced to turn the radio off altogether.

"Do you think that truck is following us?" she asks, breaking the silence. She's staring in her side mirror, chewing at her bottom lip.

I glance in the rearview mirror. "We're on a two-lane road. Where else is he supposed to go?"

She shrugs and perks up a bit. "You're probably right."

I readjust my hands on the wheel.

"It's just, he's been behind us for a while."

"Like I said, two-lane road. We're in the middle of nowhere."

"That's what scares me."

I straighten my back and watch the truck in my mirror alternating between the rearview and side mirror. "Well, I'm not scared."

I see her hand brace the grip on the passenger door.

"Tell you what, I'll take the next turnoff just to prove it to you."

"You should—"

"I should what?"

When I look over, her face has lost all color.

"Ashley?"

She's breathing hard and turning in her seat like she's in pain. It reminds me of several brides I've seen have panic attacks happen hours, sometimes minutes, before the ceremony. "You should be scared," she chokes out.

She covers her head and ducks, and I glance in the mirror and see why. There is a truck coming up on my left, a gun pointed out of the passenger window. He fires several rounds, and all I hear is the sound of metal on metal and Ashley's screams.

I do the only thing that makes any sense. I slam on the brakes.

"Call my brother." She fumbles with her phone. Her hands are shaking too badly to make any progress, so I press the button on the steering wheel and a ringing sound plays throughout the car.

Davis answers and Ashley is screaming and I'm trying to relay our location and evade bullets at the same time, and it all happens so fast. I spin out and slam into a tree. Airbags deploy and the speakers in the car go silent. I look over at Ashley, who is hyperventilating but alive. I listen for the truck to make a U-turn. "We have to go."

She glares at me, her eyes wide, mouth agape. "Go? Where?"

"The woods. Now!"

She doesn't move, so I point. "There."

Still nothing. She's either paralyzed by fear, stupid, or both. "You're going to have to run. And then, when you can't run anymore, you hide. Okay?"

She swallows hard and nods several times fast before attempting to open the passenger door. It doesn't budge. The realization that she's trapped makes her freeze up. I fling the driver's side door open and dash out. My left wrist hurts and I'm dizzy. But at least I am not dead.

Yet.

I motion for Ashley to follow me across the console. Then I lean in and reach for her, tugging hard on her forearm. "I'm sorry. I can't."

"Yes, you can. Come on."

"We're going to die," she cries. "Oh, my God. I'm going to die."

"You're not going to die."

"I'm not even thirty."

"And you never will be if you don't move your ass!"

I take off in a full sprint, and she follows. Slowly, and ridiculously, because she's in heels. Ashley is right. She's probably going to die, and it's all because she made the wrong choice in footwear.

I take my phone from my pocket and dial Roy. It rings, but then service drops, and the further I move into the woods, the less I can seem to get it back.

I'm running and I'm listening for the sound of a diesel motor. I'm searching for a signal. All I hear is silence, silence save for my heavy breathing and Ashley's sniveling. She repeatedly asks the same question. "Are they coming back?"

"I don't know."

This answer only makes her cry more, and the sound of her whining is making me lose focus, so I say, "I don't think so."

When I can't run anymore, I stop and rest my hands on my knees. I look at Ashley holding her shoes in her hands. "Who was that? Who was shooting at us?"

"Probably an ex-boyfriend."

Her mouth falls open. "Seriously?"

"No. Not seriously." I shrug. "How in the fuck am I supposed to know?"

"I thought you knew everybody around here."

"Well, it would have helped if I'd seen his face."

"Did you get the license plate?"

"No, I was too busy driving evasively and calling for help," I say through narrowed eyes. I massage my wrist and very seriously contemplate leaving her in the woods to be someone else's problem. "And you?"

She shakes her head slowly from side to side.

"Figures."

"Do you think they're coming back?"

"No." I glance toward the road. "At least not at the moment."

"How do you know?"

"Because if they truly wanted us dead, we would be."

CHAPTER NINE

Ruth

We sit in the woods, crouched down, our backs resting against a fallen tree for a good thirty minutes. I figure this should have given Davis enough time to get on the road and try to track us down. That or to call Roy, who will have called in backup. The car is visible from the road, so I am not concerned as to whether they'll find us. For now, we just have to stay put and wait.

Ashley, however, does not agree. She wants to go back for her phone, which she is sure will have service. Her eyes dart back and forth, nervously, no matter how many times I tell her we are safe. "Davey doesn't know how to find us..."

My brow furrows. I wonder if she hit her head in the crash. She's not the brightest to begin with, but now, not only does she sound dumb, she isn't making any sense. "My brother knows these roads like the back of his hands."

"I never told him our location."

"He knew I was making a trip to Hillsford."

Ashley swallows and shakes her head. "When I left he was asleep. I didn't want to wake him."

"So you lied to me?"

"I wouldn't call it a lie…"

"You acted like I was doing him a favor by bringing you along. And he had no idea."

Ashley starts to speak and then closes her mouth. She's silent for a long time, until finally I say, "Whatever. He'll figure it out."

I don't believe this, of course, because I could have gone anywhere. We could literally be anywhere right now.

She hops up and shakes her dress out. "I'm going back for my phone."

"They could be waiting for you," I say, with maximum disapproval. "The men in the truck." Not because I believe it, but so she'll listen to reason. There's no point in putting ourselves unnecessarily at risk when we're fine where we are. I refuse to leave the woods, while Ashley refuses to stay in them. When I tell her she can go alone, she calls my bluff, and that is how we end up making our way back toward the car.

Thankfully, when I reach the tree line just off the road, I spot a truck that has stopped. An older man climbs out of the cab and appears to be inspecting the scene. I watch as he walks to his pickup and radios for help. "I didn't think people used radios for that anymore," Ashley says, and I've never wanted to punch anyone in the throat more. This is not the first time I ask myself why I saved her, and it won't be the last.

"Cell service hardly exists out here," I tell her. "As we found out. Hence the radio."

"Do you think it's safe?" she asks with doe eyes.

"How should I know?" I have to admit at this point that I'm deliberately being difficult. I know the man, and I also know that his truck isn't the dark green pickup that forced us off the road in the first place.

Ashley starts immediately bawling. This catches the attention of Rusty Chamberlain, the old farmer who has a place on the other side of Hillford. He stands there for a moment, taking us in as we make our way toward him. When we reach the car, he takes his hanky from his shirt and hands it to Ashley.

"Lord as my witness, I sure wasn't expecting to see you tangled up in this, Ruthie Channing."

Mr. Chamberlin went to school with my parents. That puts him in his seventies. He walks hunched over, and he's thinner than he was just six months ago, but he's sharper than ever. He's also one of the few people that I still allow to call me Ruthie.

"That's funny. Because I sure as hell wasn't expecting it either," I say, wiping sweat from my brow with the back of my hand. "I appreciate you stopping."

"It's no trouble at all." He glances toward my car and nods. "Did you get any off on him?"

"No. Sadly."

He looks at me like he's almost ashamed. All I can do is shrug in response. "This isn't an action movie, Mr. Chamberlin." I motion with my thumb toward Ashley. "Plus, city girl here was hyperventilating as it was. That certainly would have put her over the edge."

"I see." He says like he doesn't see. Mr. Chamberlin was not born in a generation that sits and waits for the police to come and clean up the mess. Out here, in the middle of nowhere, he'd be waiting a long time. "Well, I know for sure your daddy taught you to be a good shot."

"Driving *and* shooting is a little different."

"Just takes a little practice," he tells me, opening the truck door. "What are you thinking? One of those road rage things or something else?"

"Oh, definitely something else."

Mr. Chamberlin wags a finger at me. "I was just testing you, Ruthie Channing. Honesty's always the best policy, isn't it?"

I don't answer, mostly because I'm watching the road. That, and I'm not sure I agree. I'd hate to lie to Mr. Chamberlin.

"I radioed Roy," he says. "He can get you towed in. I'd do it myself, but I've got an issue with a mare that needs tending to."

"Is Dr. Erichs coming out?"

"I don't know. We'll just have to see." He looks at my car and then back at me and furrows his brow. "Any idea who it was that did this?"

I shake my head. "I didn't recognize the truck."

"Didn't get the plates? Assuming there *were* plates."

Again, I shake my head.

"I see."

"I wish I knew who it was," I tell him, which is a half-truth. I don't know for sure, but I have a damn good idea.

"Oh, well. I have a feeling you'll find out soon enough."

Nothing further is said because Roy arrives then with his lights flashing and his siren blaring. He asks all the same questions Mr. Chamberlin already has, plus a few more. Roy calls out for a tow truck and then he drives us into Hillford, where Davis is set to meet us. I'm grateful he offers. I can skip the rest of the errands, but not the hardware store.

By the time we arrive, half the county has heard what happened. News travels fast in small towns and this news is especially salacious.

Ashley recants the story to one person and then a crowd gathers outside the store and it swells from two people to twenty.

Even I have to admit, she's aces at storytelling. You would have thought we were in a Bonnie and Clyde shootout, the way she tells it, rather than some asshole emptying his clip into my car, to prove a point or to send a message, which I suppose are sort of one and the same. I even say this at one point but she shushes me and says I couldn't have experienced it like she did because I was driving *and* I was on the phone. Of course, that's what it was.

Davis arrives and the two hug and embrace and she cries on

his shoulder and sobs into his chest, it's like a Cinderella story, like he's her knight in shining armor and the entire town is here to bear witness.

And that is how Ashley Parker becomes the IT girl.

It is how the whole town falls in love with her at once, and I come to hate her just a little more.

CHAPTER TEN

Ruth

B y mid-afternoon I'm home and things have settled enough that I fret about, unsure what to do with myself. I feel antsy, like I'm waiting for something bad to happen. I try to predict what that thing might be. A drive-by shooting? A sudden house fire? One thing is for sure, nothing is off-limits when it comes to the Holts. That family is capable of just about anything, so to say that I am on edge would be an understatement.

I do my best to keep busy. I try to keep both my hands and my mind occupied, but it isn't easy. There's not much left to do by the time the weekend of the festival rolls around. It's actually the opposite of what most people think. Everything that needs to be done has already been taken care of, plans made months ago, tiny details worked out.

Typically, by the time the Saturday of the festival arrives, there's a certain caliber of lightness in the air, a sense of freedom, the feeling that everyone's hard work has paid off. It's the start of summer, officially, and it's when the seasonal workers sort of take the reins and the rest of us locals sit back and enjoy the fruits of our labors.

At least in theory.

Small towns love nothing more than the keeping up of appearances, and Jester Falls is no different. This means it's never really entirely possible to let go. It means one is never truly off the clock. There's always some dark undercurrent that needs handling, something not seen with the naked eye. But that's business. That's business in this town.

Eventually, after circling each room at least twice, looking for things that need tidying or fixing, I wander out to the enclosed patio off the back of the house where boxes of champagne glasses are stacked neatly against the wall. I plop down into one of the white wicker rockers and count them out, just to be sure. Inevitably, the rental company shorts us a box every couple of weddings. The devil's in the details, so I count a second time for good measure. There's nothing like having to explain to a frazzled bride's mother that you don't have enough champagne flutes for the toast.

When I finish counting, I look out into the garden and contemplate taking out the ladder. I need a set of string lights replaced before the sun goes down, and I'm just restless enough that I consider doing it myself.

Outside, it has turned out to be a gorgeous day. Hot, but not *too* hot, thanks to a surprise morning rain. The sun plays peekaboo through the clouds, coming and going. Although, any minute now, I expect the clouds will clear out, giving way to mostly sunny skies.

The perfect day for a wedding, I say to myself, and I sound like the goddamned weatherman. That or my mother. It makes sense. The old radio in the corner has been left on and the actual weatherman is exuberantly relaying the weekend forecast in a way that feels like déjà vu.

I sweep my legs underneath me and lean back in the chair, nervously tapping my fingers on the arm of the chair as I stare out at the garden. My mother's wildflowers have perked up on account of the rain, and it makes me smile. It's been years since her passing, and yet it never fails that they come up each year. I have them tended to, but no matter how many gardeners I hire or fire, no one cares for them the way she did.

A cardinal lands on the bird feeder, the one Daddy put up the summer before he got sick. It's weathered now, and while I'm keenly aware that it may not hold out another season, I can't bear to replace it. I don't consider myself a sentimental person by nature, although I can effortlessly pretend. You have to in this business. That *is* the business to a large extent.

It's not just about the memories, though. At least not for me. To replace the bird feeder, string a new set of lights, or to redo the flowerbeds feels like moving on. It serves as a reminder that time really is marching forward. It's like a bullet train you know is coming before you've finished laying the track. My parents are dead and gone. Obviously. But that doesn't mean I am ready to admit that I, too, am aging, that everything eventually breaks down and has to be made new.

Breaking down is exactly what I fear is happening when some-thing in the garden catches my eye. The cardinal flies away. But it's not that.

It's the flash of pink followed by the blonde curls. Leaning forward, I scan the rose bushes and the lilacs. Nothing.

Then I look over at the daffodils and exhale a sigh of relief. My mind is not playing tricks on me. I am not having an episode, at least not at the moment. The shooter has not decided to show up and take aim. What has caught my eye is only going to kill me on the inside.

A little girl has wandered into my mother's garden, although I know with certainty that there are no children on the guest roster this weekend. We hardly get children at Magnolia House; this is not what you'd consider an attractive venue for children, though we do not outright mandate against it. Luckily, most parents are smart enough to read between the lines. We run a bed and breakfast with an old staircase and creaky floors. The house is full of antiques. There are no free lunches, no crib rental, no cookies and milk at sundown. Magnolia House is not exactly a child-friendly destination. We keep it this way on purpose.

And yet, that is exactly what is picking petals off my mother's flowers like it's nothing. She can't be more than four years old or so, although knowledge about children is not my strong suit. I wait, and leaning off the edge of my seat, I continue to scan the yard for the adult that has surely accompanied her. Sometimes people do that. They wander into the garden to take photos, to satisfy their curiosity, or both. It's safe to say, they do not build homes like this anymore. Magnolia House is really something to see.

But, no, I do not spot a parent. Just a little girl in a pink swim cover up, wreaking havoc on my mother's garden.

Without a second thought, I leap out of the rocker and fling the door open. This is so typical, someone destroying what isn't theirs to destroy for the simple fact that they can. "Hey!" I shout. "What do you think you're doing?"

The little girl turns slightly, her curls flying in the wind, dancing in place. She eyes me up and down, ultimately deciding that I am not worth listening to. I can tell by the way she goes on plucking the black-eyed Susans. "Where's Ashley?" she calls over her shoulder.

"Where are your parents?"

She spins on her heel, rotating a full circle and giggling all the while. If something is funny, I am not sure what it is. Then she says, "You're not Ashley."

I take several strides in her direction, but she's quick. "Hey! Did you hear me? I said—where are your parents?"

She reaches the rose bushes, where she tries to pluck a rose, and suddenly her little face freezes. She goes from all smiles to sheer terror in an instant. "Serves you right," I say.

She looks at me and then at the blood streaming down her finger and that does it. I have no doubt her wails can be heard for miles.

"Jesus, Ruth," Johnny says, flinging the porch door open. He strides across the lawn in a rather comical way. "What the hell?"

"She picked a rose." I look down at the little girl. "And roses have thorns."

She only cries louder. The entirety of her chubby face turns the color of the blood running from her hand onto my lawn.

Johnny crouches down, meeting her at eye level. He speaks in a calm manner; his voice soothes even me and it's like I don't even know who this man is. "Where's your mommy?"

The little girl points to the cherry laurel shrubs that separate our property from the house next door. Johnny takes her hand in his and inspects the cut. "Ruth, go get a Band-Aid."

"You go get a Band-Aid."

He's about to argue when a woman emerges from the bushes. "Lily!" She's taking deep strides in our direction, and she's out of breath. "Oh my God, Lily!"

When the woman reaches us, she drops to her knees. "You can't go running off like that."

The little girl's sobs come in frantic bursts. Then just as quickly as the rain came and went this morning, she stops. She holds her finger up for her mother to see.

"Oh honey," the mother says. "What have you done?"

"Only destroyed several of my flowerbeds," I say, and I can tell by the way she looks at me that isn't the answer she expected.

"Ruth," Johnny coughs.

"I'm sorry," the woman says to my brother. "I was on a call and I thought she was playing in her room."

"Nope," I say. "Not unless her room looks like my garden."

The woman pushes up to a standing position and extends her

hand. "I'm Alice." She pats the girl's head. "And this is Lily. We're renting the house next door for the summer, and this is not how we planned to meet the neighbors." She pauses, just long enough to smile. "And we're both terribly sorry for the inconvenience."

I am not expecting this response, and I don't know what to say. No one is this kind on purpose. Except in Jester Falls. When they have something to hide.

"It's no trouble," Johnny tells her. "No trouble at all." He too pulls himself up to a standing position, so we're all just standing there face to face, unsure of what to say. "You'll have to forgive my sister for being brash. She doesn't mean it."

"Yes, I do."

Johnny is looking at Alice, and Alice is looking at Lily, and Lily is looking at me.

"You must be one of those women my daddy is always talking about," the little girl says. Her mother's eyes widen and her mouth falls open. The little girl sniggers. "The nasty kind."

Johnny snorts. The girl peers at me with a blank expression. Her mother looks mortified.

I do a double-take. "The what?"

"I'm so sorry," the woman says before she takes her daughter by her non-bleeding hand and practically drags her across the yard. "Come on. We'd better get this cleaned up."

When the two of them reach the cherry laurels, the woman stops and looks back.

Johnny offers a wave and his signature grin. "Don't even think about it. She's wearing a wedding band," I say under my breath.

He shrugs. "So? What's that got to do with me?"

The woman listens as the girl points and then says something in protest. Finally, she turns and calls over her shoulder, "Again, I'm really sorry."

"You should be," I shout back. "We have a wedding tonight, and we can't have some toddler destroying the backdrop."

CHAPTER ELEVEN

Ruth

I'm going to put up a sign. I've fully decided. A sign that says *keep your kids to yourself,* and I'm going to stick it in the yard at the property line. I'll have it custom made at Willy's in town, so it looks nice. I have no idea if the girl is even old enough to read, and then I realize I don't care. If that doesn't work, I'll look into getting an electric fence.

The last thing I need running around here is a reminder of what I can't have.

"Ruth?" I'm spraying blood off the cobblestone when Davis comes 'round and asks if the house feels hot to me. His face is worse than it was last night, and that is saying a lot. He's worried in a way that makes him look bone tired and thin. I imagine Johnny laid into him good after what happened with the truck. He blames the Holts, which means he blames Davis for beating up Bobby Holt. By doing so, he put the rest of our lives in danger. I feel for Davis; the guilt is written all over his face. I wonder if he's okay. But I know better than to ask. "What do you mean hot?" I imagine the house going up in flames.

"Hot," he says. "As in the air conditioner isn't working."

"How would I know? I'm outside."

He drops his head back and looks up at the sky. "I see that, Ruth. I'm asking if you noticed anything."

"Yeah. First, my car got shot up, and I nearly died. Then I got trapped in the woods with Ms. America, which I wouldn't recommend. She's not the outdoorsy type. Then, as if that wasn't enough, some kid tore up the garden. And now, I'm cleaning up her mess."

"Lily, right?"

"How'd you know?"

"We met her this morning. Ashley invited her over."

"She what?"

"Hypothetically, Ruth. She invited her over hypothetically."

"It didn't look very hypothetical when she was pulling up Mama's hydrangeas."

"Anyway—the AC. Any idea how long it's been since it has blown cool air?"

"Probably since 1967."

He rolls his eyes. It's kind of pathetic, seeing that one of them is still swollen shut. "Forget it," he snaps. "I'll ask Johnny."

"Davis?"

His back straightens before he pauses and turns. "Yeah?"

"Without air conditioning, we're going to be in bad shape."

"I know that, Ruth." He says it in his usual confident way, but I wonder if he does know. There are caterers to assist and floral deliveries and a ton of things to do to make sure everything unfolds as it should. Davis never handles any of it. This is the happiest day of someone's life, or at least it's supposed to be. My job is to make sure it's not our fault if it isn't.

"Come on," Davis waves. He turns off the water at the spigot. "The sidewalk is clean, and we're going to need an extra hand."

I don't believe him. I think what he wants is an intermediary, and just like Mama, and apparently everyone else in this town, I'm a sucker where Davis is concerned, and so I go.

———

"I HATE WEDDINGS," JOHNNY COMPLAINS. I CAN'T SAY I BLAME HIM. The sun is high overhead, and it's sweltering out. He's leaning over an air conditioner unit with a wrench in one hand and a YouTube video playing on Davis's phone in the other. Johnny thinks he can handle everything himself, and at the same time, he's pissed about having to help. His little brother insinuating he needs a YouTube tutorial is one more nail in the coffin.

Davis should know better. Johnny's an expert in all things, and he's about to make the rest of us pay for the fact that we can't see it.

"They rake in the money though, weddings do," Davis says. "And God knows we need it."

I say nothing because this is a conversation I don't want to have. I already know where everyone stands on the matter. Each time it comes up, an argument ensues, and then no one speaks to each other, except that living in such close quarters and running a business you can't really help it. The subject is like lighting a stick of dynamite and waiting around for it to explode.

"Where's Ashley?"

Davis glances at me sideways. "She's taking a nap."

"She seems awfully tired all the time for someone who doesn't seem to do much."

"Maybe you should try it," Davis says. "It might make you a bit more pleasant to be around."

I cut to the chase. "I wish you hadn't brought her here."

"You've made that quite clear."

"I have a bad feeling about it."

"You have a bad feeling about a lot of things, Ruth."

"No, I don't."

"Yes, you do," Johnny agrees, which I have to say stings. He usually stays out of it. I assume he's bitter about being elbow deep in the AC unit, so I try not to take it personally.

Johnny wipes sweat from his brow. Then he looks from me to Davis. "Ruth is having one of her episodes."

I ignore him. Episodes are what the men around here call things they don't want to deal with. "She said she's a kindergarten teacher…"

Davis grins. "Yeah, so?"

Johnny furrows his brow. Even he looks surprised. This gives me a hint of satisfaction, or at the very least the will to go on. "Is she even old enough?"

"Don't be catty, Ruth."

"I think you should ask her to leave. At least until we get this thing sorted out with the Holts. I'm sure you wouldn't want her to get hurt."

"Like I would let that happen."

"They won't give up, you know. Not until they get their revenge."

Tires crunching gravel steal my attention and the chance of getting a response.

"Must be Cole," Johnny says.

"Speaking of Cole—" Davis hands Johnny a Phillips head. He's looking at me. "Don't you think you might wanna get a move on, Ruth?"

"I'm good."

"Your clock's a-ticking. If you want kids."

I rip the towel I have thrown over my shoulder and throw it at his face. "Why would I?" I motion from him to Johnny. "I already have two."

I storm off. I don't want to give him the satisfaction, but at the same time, he's hit a nerve, and some things are instinctual.

CHAPTER TWELVE

Ruth

The sun sinks low in the sky, and it's turned out to be a gorgeous evening. A cool ocean breeze peppers the air, and it's clear out. Later, a gaggle of stars will be scattered across the sky. It's the perfect backdrop for a wedding. The bride and groom say their vows under huge oaks with lights strung across the garden in front of four hundred of their closest friends and family, and it looks like something straight out of Home and Garden magazine. It's stunning.

It feels like I'm finally doing something right in my life, as though providing exceptional weddings for other people will somehow make up for the fact that I'll probably never have one of my own.

It's not that I don't want to get married. It's just that I can't get married to the person that I want.

Ashley and Davis are here, as is Cole. Roy stops by, but thankfully his appearance is short-lived as a call comes in about a group of inebriated teenagers causing trouble down at the beach. Johnny is in attendance too, with a date who isn't the usual.

She keeps giving Ashley the stink-eye, and I swear she must be the only person in this town, aside from me, who isn't falling all over themselves in order to get close to her.

Even I have to admit, she looks perfect. I wouldn't have thought one could find a dress of that caliber on such short notice, here in Jester Falls, but Ashley proved me wrong. Although, I suppose she could wear a paper sack and still look like she stepped out of the Golden Age of Hollywood. It isn't fair. Everyone wants to know where she got her dress. When Ashley tells them she got it at Anita's boutique, she and Anita become fast friends, and Anita doesn't like anyone.

"I take it you don't like this one either," Cole says.

"I just don't understand what he was thinking, bringing her here."

"Look at her," he nods. "That's what he was thinking."

"I am looking at her."

"You never like any of his girlfriends, Ruth."

"Yeah, well, I especially don't like this one."

"I wouldn't worry too much."

"And why is that?"

He takes a sip of his beer. "Men never want what they already have."

I think about this for a long moment, and I wonder if Ryan feels that way about his wife. It's been a long time, and I wonder when is the appropriate time to give up hope?

Most everyone in this town would say it doesn't matter. He cheated, and cheaters get what they deserve. I'd like to believe that were true, but I've seen too much to the contrary.

I search for Ashley Parker in the crowd and finally spot her on the dance floor. "I wouldn't say he has her. At least not the way he thinks he does." I motion with my head, and Cole's eyes follow mine. "Mark my words. That woman is going to hurt him. She's evil."

"It's tempting to see your enemies as evil. But there's good and bad on every side."

I take the bottle from his hand and toss it in the trash. "Who knew this stuff made a philosopher out of you?"

He smiles. "How are you doing?"

I know what he's asking, and it's a loaded question. "I'm fine."

"And?"

"And what?"

"Never mind." He turns to face me and then scoffs. "Someone shot up your car and ran you off the road. But you're fine. Why wouldn't you be?"

"My brothers think Bobby Holt had something to do with it..."

Cole looks at me sideways. "And you don't?"

"I don't know. I think it has something to do with that woman." I point toward the dance floor. He follows my finger until his eyes land on Ashley.

I study his face as he sucks his bottom lip between his teeth. When he releases it, he sighs heavily and looks me straight in the eye. "You don't get it, do you?"

"Get what?"

"Bobby Holt's family is asserting—" He pauses and looks away, toward the beach. "His mother spoke to Gina, at the paper—"

"Your ex-girlfriend?"

"Gina, at the Gazette."

"Yeah, your ex."

"Whatever—she said Bobby Holt's mother wants charges filed against Davis for assaulting her son. She thinks the police are looking at the wrong person in the Jenkins' investigation."

"I couldn't care less what that woman thinks. That entire family is nuts. And anyway, it wasn't an assault. It was a fight."

I watch Davis standing at the edge of the dance floor. Half of me feels sorry for him, the other half of me is furious at him for not thinking this through. He never thinks things through.

"Either way," Cole says. "She's asserting that your brother is a violent criminal, and she wants it in print."

"Anything to take the attention off the fact her son is a rapist."

"Is *allegedly* a rapist. Maybe."

"Semantics."

"That's not all. She's threatening to sue your family, Ruth."

"So let her," I scoff. The words sound brave as I say them, and yet I can't deny the sinking feeling inside.

"Gabby Jenkins told the police she never saw her attacker. So, if it was Bobby Holt, she isn't saying."

"That doesn't make any sense."

"It's common," he offers, cautiously. He holds his hands up, palms facing me. "Just don't shoot the messenger, okay?"

"So...what..." I say, changing the subject. "You and Gina... You're seeing each other again?"

"Not really." He crosses the porch and grabs another beer from the ice bucket. "Just sometimes here and there."

He pops the cap and holds the bottle out to me. "Care for one?"

"No."

I watch his mouth as he takes a long pull off the bottle. It shouldn't turn me on, considering what he's just told me. But it really, really does. What can I say? I'm a sucker for a good punch in the gut. Whatever it takes to make me feel something.

"Gina called me on account that the story she was writing had something to do with Davis."

"Right."

Cole grins. He stares at me for a long second, a strange look on his face. "Are you jealous, Ruth Channing?"

"Fuck off."

"What am I supposed to do? It's not like I can wait around forever."

"No one asked you to."

CHAPTER THIRTEEN

Ruth

The conversation with Cole bothers me enough that I go into full-on hermit mode, retreating to the kitchen. Not that it's truly possible to hide at an event with hundreds of people, but nevertheless I try.

I'm in the kitchen simultaneously hiding and pretending to search for the extra cake cutter when I hear a commotion outside.

I stretch on my tippy-toes, straining toward the window, trying to see through the crowd. A sick feeling tugs at my gut. I rush out onto the enclosed patio, navigating around guests and caterers, holding trays.

When I reach the door, my pulse quickens. What I see brings up a mixture of panic and despair. Davis has his fist raised in midair. He's straddling someone, and they are tussling on the ground, shuffling back and forth. Flinging the screen door open, I break out in a full sprint in their direction, all the while my eyes search the crowd for Johnny.

When I reach the two of them, I part the crowd. "Davis!" I shout, but it's useless. My voice is drowned out by cracking sounds, fists slamming into bone, the kind of sounds I hope to never hear again.

At some point, someone pulls Davis off. Under him, bleeding on the ground, is a kid. Not an actual kid, but a young man. Maybe twenty. Then I realize who he is. Danny Vera. The bride's brother. He stands and brushes himself off, acting as though he isn't hurt, but when he steps forward, it is with a limp.

Julia rushes in to fix things, to get everyone's attention. "It's time to cut the cake," she exclaims, and just like that the party resumes. A tinge of embarrassment fills the air, in the way that people want to gloss over what has just occurred, pretending it never happened, all the while salaciously recanting their versions of the story over half-empty champagne flutes.

The band plays a different tune.

Davis stands next to me, rubbing at his bandaged hand. Ashley checks him over, fawning like a mother hen.

"To the kitchen," I say, taking the sleeve of his shirt. "Now."

He follows me, Ashley follows him, and the door hasn't even slammed shut before I lay into him.

"What in the fuck was that about?" I grab a bag of frozen peas from the freezer and toss it onto the table. "Never mind. I'm not sure I want to know."

"That little prick grabbed my fiancée's ass. What did he expect was going to happen?"

"Your *who?*"

Ashley Parker holds out her left hand. "We were going to tell you."

"You hardly know her."

"Ruth." He holds up one hand. It's covered in blood that isn't his. "Not now, okay?"

"We're going to have to refund them their money."

"I'm sure we can work something out," Ashley says. "I mean, if we explain what happened—"

"There is no we," I say, crossing the kitchen. "In fact, this is all your fault."

"Ruth!" Davis bangs his fist on the table. "That's enough."

"This is the last thing our family needs."

Johnny walks through the kitchen doors. He's flanked by Cole.

"He put his hands on her." Davis pleads his case before the question has even been asked. "What was I supposed to do?"

"He's drunk," I say. "Like half the people here."

Davis shakes his head. "You know, for a woman, you're really something, Ruth. Like that's some kind of excuse."

"Did you have to go and beat the shit out of him?" Cole asks, coming to my aid. "In the middle of his sister's wedding?"

"You could have waited," Johnny agrees. "At least until they'd cut the cake."

"They're staying here tonight," I say. "The whole family. The kid included."

Davis shakes his head. "He's not a kid."

"He's my age," Ashley interjects.

"He called her a whore. Grabbed her ass and called her a whore. All because she refused a second dance." Davis slides a chair across the floor and takes a seat. "Forgive me for not keeping his drink filled and giving him the special turndown service before sending him on his merry way."

"What's the special turndown service?" Ashley asks, glancing around the room.

I brace myself, gripping the edge of the counter. "Seriously? *This* is the best you could do?"

"That's enough, Ruth." Johnny glares at me. "Go speak to the family. Let me handle the rest."

I throw my hands up. "What am I supposed to say?"

"I'm sure you'll figure it out."

Cole swings the kitchen door open and motions for me to follow him. "Come on, I'll go with you."

When I dig my heels in, he walks over, takes me by the hand and leads me through the house, deftly weaving around guests. When we reach the front porch, he pulls me to the side and lowers his voice. "What the hell has gotten into Davis?"

"He's *engaged*."

Cole's brows rise. "Wow."

"I know."

"Don't worry. It'll work itself out."

"It's not the only thing. What am I supposed to say to these people?"

"The truth."

"What? That their son allegedly said something inappropriate to Ashley, and then my brother lost his shit?"

"Just say you're sorry, Ruth. Start there. The rest will come."

"This is the last thing my family needs," I say, my eyes searching his. "What am I going to do?"

He places his hands on my shoulders and looks at me with enough conviction that I almost believe him when he says, "You're going to do what you always do. You're going to fix it."

Later, I apologize to the bride and groom, and she sort of laughs me off. "My brother is an ass. Even more so when he drinks."

"Mine too."

"I wouldn't worry too much," she tells me. "My parents are furious at him. It's not the first time something like this has happened. Danny can't handle not being the center of attention."

"Anyway," her husband says, "it'll make a good story for the grandkids."

CHAPTER FOURTEEN

Passerby

It's not hard to get the bastard down to the beach. All I have to do is promise him something. Like a carrot dangling from a stick, the lure of something he wants, and that's that. Weak morals and all, but then, most people are easily swayed when they think something is about to turn out in their favor.

So, easy-peasy, I get him to meet me down at the beach, or at least who he thinks is me. There are three things you should always keep a secret: your love life, your income, and your next move. Once you lose your mystery, you can't get it back. As the saying goes, sincerity is glass, discretion is diamond.

That's what I told him anyway, in the note I left beside his bed. I added a few Xs and a few Os, and from then on, it was pretty much a done deal.

Our little night swim. Our secret rendezvous under the stars.

It sounds lovely. But it wasn't all fun and games. It takes an incredible amount of strength to hold a person under the water against their will.

Thankfully, not nearly as much to entice them to get sloppy drunk first.

If you can manage that, the rest is easy.

I did. And it was.

CHAPTER FIFTEEN

Ruth

Mama always said you can talk about anything if you do it in the right way. Daddy always said, if you can't beat 'em, you might as well join 'em. I'm beginning to think there's something to that. It was especially clear in the way the guests interacted with Ashley Parker tonight. I may not be her biggest fan. But I'll say one thing, she's good for business.

During the reception, I landed two bookings. Both for large events, and surprisingly one of them came *after* my brother's outburst.

"She brings fresh blood to this town," Georgia Adkins said. "I like her." This was right before she booked her annual lady's retreat at Magnolia House. Usually, she books the fancy resort on the bay, just out of town. She says there's more room to spread out. This time, she said she wanted to stick a little closer to home and that it was Ashley who'd convinced her. She appreciates her positivity. She thinks Jester Falls could sure use a dose of that, but I think what she really meant was me. I could use a little of that charm. And who knows? If it's that easy to earn bookings, I may just give it a shot.

Ashley finds me as I'm cleaning up outside. The reception has ended, the bride and groom have retreated to their suite, and the rest of the family is hanging out in the parlor. "Ruth?" she calls out.

She says it as though I frighten her, as though I may bite. I finish clearing beer bottles from a table. Then I glance over my shoulder, brows raised. "I'm sorry. Did you say something?"

"Do you have a second?"

I scoop trash into an open bin, so I don't answer right off. I'm expecting that she'll notice the cleanup job I have in front of me. It will be several hours before I get to sit down and rest my weary feet. It's naïve of me to think that Ashley will notice anything outside of her immediate needs, because not only does she go on, she doesn't bother lifting a finger to help. "I wanted to apologize," she says. "For what happened with Davis."

I clear a second table and move on to the next. She does not give up. She stays tight on my trail. "I know you don't like me, Ruth. And I just want to say... I'm sorry about whatever I might have done to make you feel this way."

It's hard to imagine, looking at her now, the way she is groveling about, that just an hour or so ago, people were beside themselves trying to get next to her. It was fascinating to watch, albeit rather annoying, the way she drew them to her like a magnet. Effortlessly, like she was the sun, and we were all just orbiting around her. It was really something to see. The men, of course, were particularly mesmerized, although with looks like hers, that was to be expected. The women, though. Well, that was surprising for Jester Falls. To say they typically aren't welcoming is not an exaggeration. They're polite, yes. This is a tourist town, after all. But it's not an easy in with the locals. This is a tight-knit community. They don't allow just anyone into their inner circles, and even when they do, they don't exactly embrace them with open arms. There's a bit of proving oneself that has to take place. There's a trial phase, and then you're either in or you're out. And trust me, you don't want to be out. Not if you have to stick around. It reminds me of my sorority days; it's what pledging was like.

The women in this town, well, socially, they never really mature much beyond that.

So when Ashley comes to me with an apology, fake as it may be, I decide to accept it. Perhaps there is something to be learned here. I don't know what that something is, but I feel the lesson the way you sense a thunderstorm is on the horizon. It's in the air. Change is coming, and I've got to hang on for the ride.

She backs up against the table so that she's between me and the job I'm supposed to be doing. She clears her throat. "I know you haven't particularly taken to me, but I was hoping we could be friends."

It's pitiful the way she looks at me. Not even the little brat next door was this pathetic. The most irritating thing about it all is not only is she keeping me from finishing my job, it's that Ashley Parker does not need me to like her. Everyone else has already placed their vote.

"I mean…" She flashes a shy smile. "We are going to be sisters soon enough."

"That's right," I say, as though I am just remembering their engagement. "About that? When does school start back? You have to return…when…after Labor Day?"

"September, yes. But Davey and I have been talking, and I'm not sure I'm going to be going back."

And there it is. The thunderstorm I felt coming.

"I was thinking, actually, that maybe I could help out around here."

"And what would you do?" My question is meant to be sarcastic, because she's literally standing around chit-chatting while sweat drips from my brow. But she doesn't see it. I doubt Ashley Parker has ever seen a hard day's work.

"What would I do? Oh, I don't know," she tells me with a shrug. "Anything you need me to, I guess. Wouldn't it be nice for you to have a break? Perhaps you could focus on something else for a while. Davey and I could step up to the plate and handle things for a bit."

"Or—maybe my brother could go back with you. He's always talked about getting out of Jester Falls…he really has no interest in managing the day to day stuff around here. He never has."

Her face twists in a way that says she's skeptical. "You might be surprised."

I finish filling the trash bag I'm holding and then go in search of the box that contains the rest of them. Ashley follows me like a lost puppy. When I spot the box, I grab two bags, toss one at her, and say, "I forgot, where did you say you're from?"

"New Orleans."

"Ah, that's right." I motion toward the bag in her hand and the tables that are still left to clean.

She takes a deep breath in and then slowly lets it out. It's as though she's rehearsing in her mind what to say next. "I know you're angry at Davey over what happened tonight. And I know he feels terrible, even if he won't admit it. But you didn't hear the things that guy said to me. Terrible things. I realize now that I should have let it go… Sticks and stones will break my bones and all. But still."

"Still what?"

For a split-second, she looks taken aback. Her hand flies to her chest where red splotches have crept up, and I realize her tell when she's angry. "You know what I think?"

I shrug. "I asked, didn't I?"

"I think someone really needs to break that guy's bones. I think he deserved every bit of what Davey gave him and more. I mean, maybe what happened tonight will keep him from doing the same thing to another girl, and you know, even if it's only just one— well, I'll sleep better knowing."

CHAPTER SIXTEEN

Ruth

I don't mean to do it. I mean, yeah, sure, I obviously got into my car and drove the eight miles it takes to reach his house. Even so, I did not plan on doing it. Some things you just can't help, and the occasional slip-up where Cole Wheeler is concerned seems to be a weakness I can't shake.

Cole lives in a log cabin at the end of a long dirt road on property that was once owned by his great-grandfather. It was farm land back then, that for a long time hadn't been tended to. When it was passed down to Cole, he cleaned it up and built the cabin with his own two hands.

I stand at the door for a second, and then I take a seat on the porch swing. Cole will have heard me come up the long gravel drive, and also, I can't bring myself to knock. When the door finally opens and the porch light flips on, he steps out and looks at me, almost like he isn't surprised. He is shirtless, and behind him all the lights in the cabin are turned down.

For a moment I feel stupid, like maybe there is someone else here, someone who's already beaten me to the punch of warming Cole's bed. It wouldn't surprise me. It could just as easily be Gina from the paper, or any one of his regulars. Regulars he pretends he doesn't have. Cole may be discreet, but the rest of this town likes to talk.

He pushes the door open fully, reaches out, and beckons me in. I exhale a breath I hadn't realized I was holding.

I've come for sex, and he knows this, but there's something else. Something more. I need someone to talk to. Someone who will understand. Someone who will tell me the truth.

That's the deal, even if it's unspoken. I get a friendly ear, and he gets laid.

"Wanna drink?" he asks, but that's not why I'm here, so I say I haven't got the time.

He seems in no hurry, which is pretty much Cole in a nutshell. He's never been in a hurry for anything, not in all his life, and I don't think that's about to change now. His place is neat and tidy. He doesn't own much, unless you count a lot of dusty old paperbacks. I scan one of the stacks near the fireplace. Heinlein, Levin, Orwell, Burgess, and lots of H.G. Wells. Cole's always been sort of a cowboy at heart with the brains to back it up. "Do you actually read these or are you just using 'em to keep the fire going?"

"It gets lonely out here."

"I'm sure it does." I pull several from the stack and study the covers. "Which is your favorite?"

"It's hard to choose just one. I like them all."

"I bet you do." His gaze makes me feel uncomfortable, like the room has suddenly grown ten times hotter. "But gun to your head —if you had to choose?"

He walks over and looks over what I have in my hand. "This one," he says. *"The Moon Is a Harsh Mistress."*

"Can I borrow it?"

"No."

"Seriously?"

"Seriously."

"I thought you'd do anything for me."

"That's not the same thing as giving you anything."

"Isn't it?"

Cole gives me a look. It's the same one he always gives when he's had enough conversation. He's a man of few words and has been since we were kids. I watch him closely as he puts on music, the usual old country songs that make me long for simpler times. "Do you play this for all your women?"

"Just you, Ruth Channing," he tells me in a way that almost makes me believe him.

"It's the melancholy, isn't it?"

"Come," he says, reaching for my hand. "Dance with me."

And so I do.

CHAPTER SEVENTEEN

Passerby

The wind in my hair, the spray on my face, it's really something. It feels like fast cars and freedom. Only different because I'm on a boat. I push down on the throttle, wondering if I should ease up some. I'm not really looking to draw attention to myself, and boating accidents are quite common. I looked it up just to be sure.

I slow a little, mostly because I don't know the game warden situation around here, but if I had to guess, I'd bet it's like most things in this town, fairly lame.

After bringing the boat to a standstill, I sit and listen. I take out my reel and my ice chest, putting both within eyesight, even though it's dark out. The sun is still an hour or so from rising, and it's peaceful out here on the water, but that could change in an instant. I may not be looking for company, but it's important to be prepared should any arrive.

To be completely honest, I'm only looking for one person, a

big fish in a small pond. And as luck would have it, like many people in this town, Bobby Holt is an avid fisherman. Turns out, every Saturday morning he gets up before the crack of dawn and heads out. Sometimes as early as 4:00 a.m.

Who knew I had it in me, too?

I'm learning so much.

Everything is happening exactly as it should.

New hobbies can be fun.

All I had to do was to bide my time and wait. And now, here I am.

And here he comes. The man I'm looking for.

A chance encounter. A meeting of two minds.

They'll find his boat empty and his body in the water.

Eventually.

I'll be long gone by that time. Probably off having coffee, smiling, and waiting for the story to break. I doubt it will take long. It's a small town and news travels fast.

Thankfully.

CHAPTER EIGHTEEN

Ruth

I'm up early, on account that we have a full house and there's a lot to do before the wedding party's departure. Breakfast is being catered before the big farewell send-off for the bride and groom, and it's my job to see that everything is in order.

I rub at my eyes and wish the coffeepot had a turbo speed button. I slept so little that it feels like I hardly slept at all. I'm in the kitchen waiting on the coffee to brew when the doorbell rings at the back door. Usually the bell is reserved for deliveries, but it's barely daylight out, and I'm not expecting anything this early, so this is surprising.

For a second, I consider waking Johnny, but when I part the curtains, I see Roy's cruiser outside and through the peephole, his face stares back at me.

I open the door slowly and not even all the way. At least not until his expression says he's coming in. "What is it?"

"Can I come in?" His eyes shift. "I'm afraid I've got bad news."

"What do you mean *bad news?*" My voice comes out high-pitched and shrill. I try to play it off like I'm calm, but it's very apparent I am not.

Roy eyes me up and down. "You might want to put some clothes on for this."

"I have clothes on."

"No, I mean like real clothes. There's about to be a lot going on here."

"Just tell me. What is it?"

"We found Danny Vera down at the beach."

"Okay?"

"Someone jogging found him. He's dead, Ruth."

"Dead?" I shake my head from side to side, like I can shake off what he has just said. "I don't understand."

I say the words. But I do understand, and everything is coming slowly even though all the information is being delivered at once.

"His parents?" Roy asks, glancing up at the ceiling. "They're here, right?"

"Yes," I say. "Upstairs."

He nods knowingly. "You'd better go wake them."

I feel sick. At any minute I'm going to be sick. "Do I have to?"

"Yes, Ruth. Unfortunately, you do."

"Can I have coffee first?" I ask the question as though I am not a free woman in my own home. The words coming out of my mouth do not sound like my own. I do not feel like coffee, but I also do not feel like waking anyone and telling them their son is dead.

"Make it quick."

I grab a mug—my favorite mug—from the cabinet and fill it with coffee I do not intend on drinking. I just need a moment.

"Ruth," he says, sternly. "This place is about to be swarmed by people. I'm going to need you to get a move on."

I take one sip of the black coffee, knowing it's pointless. Even if I managed to force it down, it wouldn't stay that way. "Okay," I tell him, willing my pulse to settle down. "Let me get dressed."

Roy waits while I throw on a pair of jeans and pull a sweater over my pajama top. When I come back into the kitchen, he's standing in front of the window, looking out. He turns to me and suddenly he's not the kid I sat next to in kindergarten, or the boy I kissed in the third grade. He's all business. "Bring them into the living area and have them sit down."

DANNY VERA'S MOTHER'S WAILS CAN BE HEARD FROM SEVERAL blocks away. When Roy tells the couple their son has been found dead, she first turns to her husband. Her mouth is poised to speak, although words do not come.

She sinks from the couch to her knees. Her expression morphs from shock to despair, and then she screams. It's guttural and horrific, the kind of sound you know you're never going to forget. I hadn't woken her daughter or her son-in-law, or any of the other members of the family. I realize now this was a mistake. There's no way they're sleeping through this, and it's not a very pleasant way for them to find out.

Mr. Vera holds his wife, and as he rocks stoically back and forth, Roy rattles off a series of questions. "Did Danny have any medical issues?"

Mr. Vera shakes his head.

"Did he mention he was going down to the beach? Was he a runner?"

No. And not really.

"How much had he had to drink? Did he have a history of drug use?"

It's around this time his sister appears, sleepy-eyed and

disheveled. She requested a 7:00 a.m. wake-up call so as not to miss their honeymoon flight. This is not the wake-up call she expected, and I feel terrible for her. Memories of her wedding will always be marked by tragedy.

I can't imagine losing one of my brothers.

Speaking of, Johnny is the first to come to my aid. He's in his fire department gear. He looks exhausted, but his presence brings a certain sense of calm. I haven't given any thought about what is to come next, not until Ashley enters the room, with Davis just a few steps behind her. They look at me, their faces full of questions. They don't know what's going on, other than it isn't good and that's when Mrs. Vera changes, like in the movie *The Exorcist*. She goes from a grieving mother to looking like that little girl with her head spinning round and round in an instant. It shocks everyone when she points at Davis, even Roy, and nothing surprises him. She extends her arm all the way out.

"You!" she shouts, as spittle flies from her lips and snot bubbles from her nose. "This is all your fault!"

Ashley looks stricken, and Davis's expression is marred in surprise. "You humiliated my son!"

Her husband tries to calm her. He smooths her hair, whispering vacant words into her ear, but it doesn't work. She is hell-bent on getting out what she has to say. "You assaulted Danny," she says, with a level of venom I'm not sure I've ever seen. "And now he's dead."

"What?" Davis asks, looking at me.

I nod confirmation. He has just heard her correctly.

Ashley gasps and then covers her mouth with her hand.

Mrs. Vera sobs. When Davis moves to leave the room, she lunges at him. Roy catches her by the forearm as though he saw her next move before she did. He stays behind with the family as the three of us make a speedy exit. We congregate in the kitchen, and after we've caught our collective breaths, I ask what the hell just happened, even though it's pretty clear.

"I don't know," Davis answers solemnly. He takes a seat at the table, the same one he sat in as a little boy. He leans forward and rests his elbows on the table. He looks from me to Ashley as though he wants to say something, but isn't sure what. Finally, he places his face in his hands and he looks like he did as a child, only larger. Ashley stands over him with a worried look on her face. She rubs circles on his back as she stares off into space. "This isn't your fault, Davey."

"His mother's just upset," I say. "Understandably so. People always look for someone to blame in times of tragedy. It's just the way it goes."

I pour four cups of coffee that none of us touch. None of us except Ashley.

Standing on my tiptoes, I look out the window toward Daddy's old workshop, which Johnny has claimed and transformed into his living quarters. The light is on.

Sometimes I pull up Magnolia House on Google Maps Street View. The image was taken in 2012. There's a light on in the workshop. It is still Daddy's favorite place to be. He is still alive. I am still visiting every few months, making the trip home from college. Mama's car is still in the drive, but Davis will pick me up at the bus station, and when we arrive, she will be standing in the doorway, waving, looking older and thinner than the last time I saw her. We will watch old movies, and sit in the garden, and there will have been no scary diagnosis, no utterance of the c-word, and Daddy's heart would still be ticking just fine. And I won't know how perfect it is, or that I will learn that sometimes it's best not to know. I keep several screenshots in various places of that image of the workshop with the light on because it won't last forever. One day the Google car will drive back down this street and his workshop will not be his workshop anymore, and though there may be a light on, it won't be him.

"What do you think, Johnny?" He's scrolling on his phone and although he hears me, he doesn't immediately respond. "Huh?" He doesn't even look up. "I don't know. Give me a sec."

Davis shakes his head. "This is not good," he says, with a heavy sigh. He looks panicked, like he wants to get up and run. "I—"

"We don't know how Danny Vera died. People die every day. It could have been anything."

"It doesn't seem like they think it was natural causes," Ashley says. "Based on what I overheard."

My head snaps from the window to her. "And what was that?"

"You know—" She nods toward Davis with wide eyes and a concerned expression on her face. She places her index finger to her lips, like a warning. "Just gossip."

Outside, the caterers have begun to arrive. I don't know whether to send them away or not. I don't know what the family wants me to do. Surely, no one will feel like eating. But eventually, they'll have to.

"Someone has to know something," Davis remarks.

"It'll take at least six weeks for toxicology to come back," I say, and the conversation continues, even though we only talk in circles. The three of us speak in unison, talking over each other, our voices growing louder and louder in the fight to be heard. Then Johnny holds his hand up, and we all suddenly fall silent. "Ruth, you need to call Mike."

Ashley looks at me. "Who's Mike?"

"Our family attorney," Davis replies flatly.

I know he is right, but I want to see where his head is at. "He didn't die on our property."

"He was a guest." Johnny glances toward Davis. "And his mother keeps bringing up what happened last night. The situation between him and Davis."

I nod at his phone. "Did you get called to the scene?"

"Yes. Initially."

What he means is he got the initial call but when he got there, it was clear there was nothing he could do. Still, I can tell Johnny knows more than he's saying. He's processing. And Johnny always goes quiet when he's in process mode. Not that I blame him. I know he sees a lot. That and anything to do with law enforcement, and, well, they all talk. "What are they saying?"

"No obvious signs of trauma."

I close my eyes and I exhale. "At least there's that."

CHAPTER NINETEEN

Ruth

The Vera family packed up and quickly vacated the premises. This was both good news and bad. Good, because it's awful dealing with a bereaved family. Bad, because it shows they're, at least to some degree, placing blame on my family for their son's death.

After their departure, I spend a good part of the day helping Julia clean and overturn the rooms for the guests who are set to check in this afternoon. Roy's partner removed Danny Vera's belongings from his room. She spent a good hour in there, doing I'm not sure what. Obviously she was searching for something, a suicide note possibly, or some other clue as to what might have happened. Otherwise healthy twenty- somethings rarely drop dead without warning. All I know is we are fully booked tonight, which means the opportunity to sit around and ponder the situation is short-lived. There are things that have to be done, and it's just me and Julia to handle them.

Johnny's busy with the fire department.

Davis is busy with Ashley.

Ashley's busy with… well, that's a good question.

I'm busy trying to keep us in business.

I haul the trash from the kitchen out to the large bins we store behind the workshop, and as I head back to the house to finish folding the last of the linens, I'm making a mental list of what's left to do. As I round the corner to the front of the house, I stop in my tracks. I am not expecting to see the squad car in the drive or Roy standing next to Davis's truck inspecting the tires. "Can I help you?"

"Ah, Ruth," he says, bending upward from the waist. "I was hoping you might be around."

When am I not? The words almost roll right off my tongue. I bite them back because it's none of his business. This, and he keeps asking me for a date.

"We're booked," I say. "Tonight. And there's still lots to do yet…" I am hoping that he'll take the hint. I don't have time to hang around making small talk.

Roy places his hands on his hips. "Aren't you always?"

"What?"

"Aren't you usually booked solid?"

"This time of year, yes. But with everything this morning— well, I got a late start on turning the rooms over. And now you're back." My response comes out harshly, but I can't help it. I'm annoyed that I have to repeat myself, plus there's the overwhelm. All it takes is one or two negative reviews and business can dry up like that. I've seen it happen. Hospitality is a precarious industry, and attention to detail is important. There's no half-assing cleanliness. Still, he doesn't take the hint.

He passive aggressively refuses to get to the point and let me get on with my day. Of course he does. In this town, he has nothing better to do, and his uniform makes people feel obligated to entertain his whims.

This is why I change course. I subtly remind him that there are things to do other than to hang around my place, groveling for a date he'll never get. I am not, nor have I ever been, attracted to Roy. "How's Gabby Jenkins?"

Roy knows exactly why I'm asking about Gabby. He's a cop through and through, which means he's aware I'm fishing for info on her father. Not that I care what Roy thinks. I'm not trying to hide it. I'm trying to kill two birds with one stone. "She's...um... you know... She's recovering."

"That's good."

He looks me dead in the eye. "He cheated on you, Ruth. Ages ago. And here you are, still moping around, pining over him."

"No, I'm not. I'm working."

"Do you think Ryan Jenkins is concerned about you? Has he ever once called? Has he ever once shown interest? In all these years?"

I don't answer his line of questioning. I know good and well when to keep my mouth shut, but yes, Ryan Jenkins did call me once. The night before he got married. Sure, he was drunk. But he called. He said a lot of things that showed concern. But mostly, he wanted to know if I could forgive him.

Supposedly, what happened was a one-time thing. A one-time thing that resulted in a pregnancy. I'll never know whether or not that's true, I only know it doesn't really matter. What happened *happened*, whether he messed up one time or twenty.

He ended up with a wife and a daughter.

Either way, I could have forgiven him. Or at least I think I could've. Maybe I should have told him as much. But I was bitter, and more than that, I was embarrassed. Heck, some would argue I'm still bitter. We were supposed to go to college together, to come back to Jester Falls afterward, get married and raise a family. Ryan hit the fast forward button on life, and he did it with someone else. But even that's not why I lied.

I lied because I thought he'd keep trying. I didn't know that if I told him I couldn't—in any way, shape, or form—get past what he'd done, that he'd go ahead with the wedding. I was young and immature. It was a long time ago, back when I thought that if you loved something, that if you loved *someone*, you fought for them. Maybe there's a part of me that still thinks that, and maybe that is the part of me that is asking Roy how Ryan is, without actually asking. Maybe, I've come to realize, it's better to have a thing than not.

"Anyway," Roy tells me with a disappointed sigh. "I'm here about what happened at the Holts' place the night before last."

"And what's that?"

"Come on, Ruthie. Don't play dumb with me." He shifts his weight from one foot to the other. "You're a lot of things, but we both know you're not that."

"Don't call me Ruthie. We're not kids anymore."

"No, we aren't."

We stand there for a bit, like we're having a moment of silence for our youth. Finally, he glances around the property. "Say, is Davis around?"

"No, he went into town."

Roy looks at me funny. "Hmmm."

He shields his eyes from the sun and then motions with his thumb toward the driveway. "Isn't that his truck?"

"He took one of the others."

A sly grin edges across his features, and then he cocks his head. I know this look well. He's about to test his authority. "You wouldn't be lying to a police officer, would you, Ruth?"

I shrug. "I'm not under oath. And I'm not lying."

"I heard that Holt boy was in pretty bad shape the other night."

"Yeah, well, so was Gabby Jenkins."

He juts out his bottom lip to indicate a fair point has been made. "You wouldn't have thought he'd get up and go fishing this morning, but he did."

"So obviously he wasn't in that bad a shape. And what's that got to do with Davis?"

"Nothing, I hope."

"Well, then why are you here?"

"Bobby Holt was found dead this afternoon, Ruth. And his family doesn't think it was an accident."

CHAPTER TWENTY

Ruth

Cole comes straight over when I call. I'm sitting on the porch where Julia has brought out tea and her famous pimento cheese dip. She's beside herself over what happened with the Vera family, and she tries to remedy her anxiety by making sure everyone is taken care of and then some. It's the sweetest kind of overkill the way she hovers. It reminds me of my mother. I don't fault her for it. Julia is the best thing that's ever happened to this family. She loves us like we are blood, through thick and thin. She takes it personally when something goes wrong with a guest; she lives to make them happy, so the death of one is weighing heavily on her heart.

Cole stops as he always does and dusts his boots on a mat at the bottom step. When he looks up, he says, "I take it you heard about Bobby Holt."

"At this point, everyone has."

As he climbs the steps, I take the opportunity to admire him.

The broad shoulders, the thickness of his arms, his easy smile. He walks over and stands next to me, resting his back against the pillar. "Is that why you called?"

The truth is, I don't know why I called Cole, and now that he's here, I'm even less sure. I only know I have the distinct inclination to drag him upstairs to what has always been one of our favorite rooms. "I guess so."

He looks me in the eye for a little too long not to have any feelings for me, and then he says, "Is there something else?"

Yes. Yes, there is. "Ruth?"

I can't seem to spit the words out. But then I realize I'd better get it over with. "Roy practically came straight here. He seems to think my brother had something to do with Bobby's death..."

Cole looks at me sideways. "Johnny?"

"No, Davis."

"Is that what you think?"

What do I think? I think my biological clock is ticking and making babies with you looks pretty damn good right now. I think that would be the sweetest disaster, and though I could easily make it happen, I won't, because I'm too scared to face the fallout. "I don't think it was either of them. The Holts have no shortage of enemies."

"No," he says. "They don't. I wouldn't lose any sleep over it. My guess is, and this is just based on what I've heard, it'll probably be ruled an accident."

"Maybe."

He takes the seat next to mine. "Why do I sense there's something you want to say but aren't?"

"You tell me."

"You called me here for a reason."

He's asking in his own way if I want to go upstairs. Really, I want to go anywhere. Right here on this porch would do. But then, as with every other area of my life, there are other people to consider. Just once I'd like to know what it feels like to be selfish. I don't say any of this, of course. I just silently pray that Cole is as intuitive as I hope he is. "I think Ashley has something to do with what's going on."

I say this, and even as the words float off my tongue, I want to reel them back in. Suggesting Ashley is involved also implicates Davis.

Cole's face breaks into a wide grin. "She doesn't exactly seem like someone with the wherewithal or the know-how to commit not one but multiple murders."

"How can we ever really know what a person is capable of?"

He laughs. "You know I adore you, Ruth Channing. But I think you might be overthinking things a bit."

"Why wouldn't I be? Two men with ties to my family have been found dead within the past twenty-four hours."

"What's that saying about causation?"

"Correlation does not equal causation."

"Ah, that's right." Cole knows this.

"Don't mock me."

"I'm not mocking you. It's just that seeing two variables together does not necessarily mean we know whether one variable caused the other to occur."

"Sure, I didn't see Ashley Parker take out Bobby Holt or Danny Vera, but would I put it past her? *No.* No, I wouldn't."

He narrows his eyes. "Have you been drinking?"

"No, but I think I'm about to start."

"Good," he says, standing. He smooths his pant legs. "Mind if I join you?"

Cole opens the screen door and motions for me to follow. So I do. "And if she didn't murder them, assuming they *were* murdered, I think she sure as hell knows who did," I tell him between gritted teeth as we make our way to the kitchen. "Obviously, I have no proof of this. Just a feeling in my gut."

"Is that right?"

"Yeah, but I don't have to understand it intellectually. I just know it. Plus, what more evidence do I need? I heard it straight from the horse's mouth. She said: *Someone really ought to take care of him...* Then, about Danny Vera she told me: *I think someone really needs to break that guy's bones. I think he deserved every bit of what Davey gave him and more."*

Cole takes the bottle of tequila from the liquor cabinet. "If that doesn't look damning, I don't know what does."

I can't tell whether he's joking or not. "I only know it wasn't my brother."

God, I hope it wasn't my brother.

"It wasn't your brother," he says, filling two glasses. He hands one to me. "Either of them."

It couldn't have been. *Could it?* I don't say this out loud. It feels bad enough just thinking about it.

Cole sucks in his bottom lip and then releases it. I can tell what he's thinking.

"What?" I ask.

He glances at his watch and then looks at me in a way that tells me he doesn't want to say what's on his mind but he knows he has to. "I'm not sure I want to get into this right now but..."

"But what?"

"This makes two women asserting their son's death had something to do with Davis."

"Yeah," I scoff. "I thought that was established..."

"Have you called your attorney?"

"I'm waiting for him to call me back."

"You should put in another call. I wouldn't wait."

"This isn't Davis's fault. None of it."

"Hey, I said that already," he tells me, holding his hands up in defense. "Now we're just talking in circles, and besides, I'm not the one you need to convince."

I look at him, tilt my head, and narrow my eyes. "There's something you're not saying."

He hesitates for several long beats before he says, "Bobby's mother called Gina again."

I down my glass in two quick gulps and then slam it on the counter. Cole didn't want to have this conversation because he knew if he did, he wouldn't get laid. And this is why we can't have nice things. This is why I can't have a child that shares half of his DNA. I can't trust him. "How much does Gina know about you and me?"

"What is that supposed to mean?"

"It means what it means."

"Why are you asking me that?"

"Why are you evading the question?"

I cross the kitchen, take the bottle of tequila from the counter, and refill my tumbler. "I'm just wondering why she might have a reason to have it out for my family. Now, it makes sense."

"I'm not the enemy here, Ruth. And believe it or not, not everyone is out to get you."

"So you're defending her then?"

"I'm not defending anyone. Gina's a member of the press. She has a story to tell."

"Never mind if it's a lie."

Cole places his glass in the sink and turns on the tap. It's his way of checking out of the conversation. It's his way of telling me he's about to walk in and out of my life.

I grab the bottle of tequila from the counter and take a long pull on the bottle. "Tell her she can have you, I'm done."

"I think you're overreacting. This isn't about me."

"Sure it is."

"What's that supposed to mean?"

"You don't know women at all."

CHAPTER TWENTY-ONE

Ruth

D ays go by, each one passing like molasses. Festival weekend comes and goes, and each day thereafter feels pretty much like the one before it. Little is said about Danny Vera. The Holts delay a funeral for their son, although eventually the gossip and speculation around that dies out, too.

As for me, I seem to get a little less jumpy and a little more melancholy with each passing day. I become less concerned that someone is going to pop up out of nowhere and shoot me dead or run me off the road and more concerned with the fact that I'm probably never going to be a mother. All of a sudden, I become more comfortable with the idea of dying. It hardly feels like I have a lot to live for. And at any rate, all I know is that I can't live at that level of alert, or stay on edge like that forever. Not without going crazy.

It's amazing how fast I adjust to this new sense of normal, even though I don't quite know what that means, other than things are different, but in many ways, very much the same as before. Ashley says that humans are wired to move past things, that it is understandable for us to want to fall back into a normal routine, and as much as I don't want to believe anything she says, I do. I fall into a routine that looks a lot like my routine every summer. Life does not stop when things get crazy. It keeps moving on past and it leaves little room for catching up, so eventually, I suppose we all just sort of let go and fall into step.

Late one evening, I'm seated at the kitchen table poring over bills and bank statements and invoices when Julia comes to me with a pained expression on her face. She's gripping her rosary beads, which is what she's always done when she has bad news to deliver. "Jesus Christ, Julia," I say impatiently. "What is it?"

She eyes me hesitantly.

I slap an open palm against the table. "Just spit it out, would ya?"

I don't mean to snap at her. I haven't been sleeping well and I'm frustrated, not the least of all reasons being that after the argument with Cole, I haven't gone out to the cabin simply as a matter of principle. And aside from all of that, I hate accounting. Nothing is adding up, and what the numbers show is not what I was hoping to see. For a bed and breakfast that is always booked, it seems our margins are very thin. Money seems to be seeping out from many angles and much faster than we're bringing it in.

Julia looks at me suspiciously, like I have lost my mind. "You should not use the Lord's name in vain."

"I'm not," I say, punching numbers into the calculator. "I'm calling upon him to help you get the words out."

"Ah, Ruthie." She shakes a finger at me. "Your mama would have soap in your mouth if she were here. You remember? Like the good old days."

"The good old days, yes. Funny, I recall them a bit differently."

I jot the figure down on the paperwork in front of me, and

then I look up. "I'm sorry," I sigh. "Whatever it is you have to say, I doubt it could be worse than this."

She looks worried, and I instantly wish I could take the words back. I try to think of ways to tell her that her job is safe, without making things even worse, but I can't seem to come up with anything.

"Soap in your mouth," she tells me. "That is worse than this, no?"

Poor Julia. I think my punishment was harder on her than it was on me. She used to feel so bad that Mama would make me sit in the bathroom sucking on a bar of soap for the better part of an hour. This was back when people did things like teach their kids' lessons. I doubt the mother next door has ever thought about giving her daughter a bar of soap. It might save her some trouble down the line. But you can't tell people anything these days. It's not the parents' fault their children are assholes.

It's just that it's hard to be a decent person if you're never told the word no. Just look at the woman staying in our guest house.

"I can still taste that soap sometimes," I say to Julia, and she laughs.

It wasn't just the soap that was awful. It was being stuck in the bathroom for all that time, away from everyone. I hated every second of it. Julia used to feel so bad that she'd sneak in glasses of Kool-Aid. Other times she'd slip a handful of the mints we used to leave on guest's pillows under the door.

Mama would come in and my lips and tongue would be blood red and she'd ask when I'd gotten into Kool-Aid. She'd blame the sugar for my bad behavior and act all confused, and it was only later, much later, that I learned she never really was. Mama missed nothing that went on in this house. If only I could be more like her, then I wouldn't have to depend on Julia to deliver news she can't seem to get out.

"It's about Ms. Ashley," she says. She treads cautiously, even going so far as to wince as she speaks.

"What about her?" *God, why does everything have to be about her?*

"I found this."

She hands me a driver's license. It's from Louisiana.

"I found it in her room, in the guest house. I was cleaning." She looks sad, and I understand why. Julia has just broken one of her sacred values. She prides herself on discretion. It's the pinnacle of who she is and of her work. "I didn't want to tell Davis. I know I shouldn't pry—so I brought it to you."

"It's okay," I say. "I'm glad you did."

I glance down at the plastic in my hand. The woman in the photo staring back at me is the same woman sleeping in my guest house. But her name isn't Ashley Parker.

CHAPTER TWENTY-TWO

Ruth

I'm in the parlor refreshing the selection of magazines we keep out on the tables when Ashley enters the front door of Magnolia House. Her arms are weighed down by shopping bags, and she has a stack of packages in her hands. I watch as she dumps her haul onto the floor in the entryway, the bags slinking from her arms like a sloughing of a second skin.

"Hey," I call out. "Can you come here?"

It feels like as good a time as any to ask for the truth. Although, I haven't yet decided how to start the conversation. Do I begin with an icebreaker? Or should I just get straight to the point? *Who the hell are you? Why are you here? And what is it that you want?*

All I know is that the Ashley Parker mystery gives me a reason to want to live. It gives me a reason to get out of bed in the morning. It gives me purpose, now that Cole and I aren't speaking. I shift from having a full-on pity party to something that feels more like an intimate gathering for rage, and I have to say, it feels better.

It helps that I've kept myself busy. I've spent the past twenty-four hours making a ton of phone calls. I've searched the internet, combed through all the school websites in the greater New Orleans and surrounding areas, carefully scanned the staff profiles on each webpage, and when that didn't turn up with anything, I called.

I've tried multiple searches using the name on the driver's license, and none of them pulled up anything of interest. The search results did not get me any closer to finding out who in the hell this woman occupying my home really is.

In this day and age, I wouldn't have imagined that it would be this difficult to determine a person's identity. People post everything online. They tag their friends and relatives; they tell you what they ate for dinner and their opinions on just about everything. It leaves me baffled. But it also gives me a lot to think about. People post endlessly, but do they ever really tell you who they are?

I don't simply want to know who Ashley *is*. I want to know what she *wants*. I want to know who she is hiding from and *why* she's hiding.

I wish I could say that my mind comes up with a gazillion answers, a billion explanations, a million rationalizations, but it doesn't. The cold hard truth is I'm no closer to finding answers than I was when I started. And it isn't for lack of trying. This leaves me little choice but to go to the source, and as luck would have it, she's sashaying into the parlor wearing a grin the size of Texas.

"It's hot out," she says, pretending to wipe sweat from her brow. "I didn't know it got this hot here."

"I'm finding there are a lot of things I don't know." I toss a stack of magazines on the table. "Like really anything at all about you."

She looks at me like I'm a challenge she's excited to face. "I'm probably less interesting than you think."

"Try me."

"Of course." She picks up a magazine and studies the cover. "I'll tell you anything you want to know. But first—you're going to want to hear what happened in town. Trust me."

I don't trust her. Nor can I wait to hear what she has to say. I plop down on the sofa and fold my legs underneath me.

"There were these suits," she exclaims as she paces back and forth in front of the fireplace, and it's like all the world's her stage. When she speaks, her eyes are wild, and she gestures with her hands in a way I find confusing. "You know, like men. In actual suits."

"Okay?"

"With cowboy hats."

"Yeah? So?"

"So I struck up a conversation with one of them and guess what? They're looking to buy property here."

"Shocker."

"And I told him about Magnolia House and he seemed really interested—"

I cut her off. "Magnolia House is not for sale."

"Right. But maybe you might want to hear what he had to say. You know, just for shits and giggles."

"Shits and grins."

"Huh?"

"The saying—it's shits and grins."

She gives me this light, school girl giggle that makes me want to stab my eyeballs out as she waves me off. "Anyway, I'll come back to that—you'll never in a million years believe who I also ran into!"

"It's a very small town."

"Someone I hear is...or *was* very special to you—I don't know—you'll have to spill the tea!"

I study her curiously. She's good. I'll give her that. The suspense should be killing me, but I know exactly where she's going. She knows I know. Or at least I think I know. I can't decide which it is. And I don't think she can either.

She waits for an answer, and when I don't offer one, she throws her hands in the air like we're playing a game of charades. "Ryan Jenkins!"

"I never would have guessed."

"Wait—" She chews at her bottom lip. "Are you being serious?"

She crosses the room. "What a cutie! I mean… He sort of has the dad bod thing going, but I don't know… He's okay. Like… he's perfect for you." She nods to show that she's satisfied with herself for expressing her thoughts in such an eloquent way. "Yeah, that's it. That's what I'm trying to say."

"Ryan is married. So, no, he is not perfect for me."

"All things can be undone."

"From your mouth to God's ear," I say. She misses the point entirely.

"And anyway," she tells me, scrunching up her perfectly upturned nose. "He didn't even seem happy."

"His feelings are not my concern."

"When's the last time you spoke to him?"

"I don't know. Why?"

"Well, it's just… If you saw him, then you'd know. You'd know how he feels about you."

"It doesn't matter how he feels about me."

"Yeah, well—your body language and your brother tell me differently." She laughs like she's joking, but also like the joke is on me. "What I'm trying to say, Ruth—" She pauses and walks over to the sofa.

She sits next to me and places her hand on my knee. It feels like we're either on daytime television or she's about to deliver some really important news. Finally, through bated breath she says, "What I'm saying is you could have him if you wanted him."

"But I don't."

"Come on, Ruth. This is me you're talking to. We're practically sisters. There's no reason to lie. Not to me."

After removing her hand from my knee, I scoot off the sofa. I walk over to the large window and stand in front of it, looking out. I'm just about to tell her what I know, to demand that she tell me the truth, when she says, "I could help you, you know."

"Help me how?"

"I know a thing or two about men."

"I have no intention of breaking up a family."

"They're hardly a family." Her tone grows both desperate and excited, maybe a little frantic. "If you'd been there—if you'd seen what I'd seen, then you'd know. Look at you! You're sitting around here miserable for nothing when what you want is right there for the taking. All you have to do is reach out and grab it."

"I think you're mistaken."

"I'm not. That's what she did, isn't it? She wanted your boyfriend, and she took him. Didn't she?"

"It was a long time ago."

"You see, Ruth, that's the thing. There's no statute of limitations on revenge."

I watch out the window as the little girl next door plays in the yard. A man I assume is her father looks from the porch intermittently. Most of the time he stares at his phone.

"Don't worry, though," Ashley quips. "You'll see. Because surprise! I invited them here."

My head snaps in her direction. "Why would you do that?"

"What? It's my engagement party. I can invite who I want."

"Not them."

"Don't be silly. It'll be good for Gabby. She'll like you once she gets to know you. She'll see that this is all for the best. All you have to do is sit back and relax."

"Is there something wrong with you?"

"With me?" She touches her chest lightly and lets her hand rest there. "No. Why do you ask?"

"You sound crazy. And I think there's something you're not telling me."

"Nope," she quips. "There isn't."

"I know your name isn't Ashley."

Her head cocks, and her eyes narrow. I think she's going to say something, but she doesn't.

"Well?"

"Well, what?"

"I know you aren't who you say you are."

"No one is who they say they are." She sighs and she seems relieved. "Not even you. Haven't we established that in this conversation? You're living one big fat lie. So is Ryan Jenkins. And how funny that you have it in you to point fingers at others."

"I'm going to tell Davis."

"What makes you think he doesn't already know?"

"I—"

"I'm not one to be messed with," Ashley says, cutting me off. "If there's anything you should know, it's that."

"Are you threatening me?"

"No," she tells me. "Of course not."

"Because I find it interesting that since you showed up, men around here seem to be dropping like flies."

"I have nothing against women." She flashes a wicked smile.

"I don't think you know as much about me as you think you do."

"I know enough." She leans forward and checks her reflection in the mirror over the mantle. "Any-who, the party is a week from tomorrow. I checked the calendar in your office." Her eyes meet mine. "It's a Sunday, which wasn't ideal. But what is it they say? Beggars can't be choosy?"

"We're not having a party."

"Don't be difficult, Ruth. All you have to do is put on a nice dress, sit back, and look pretty. That shouldn't be too hard, should it?"

"Who's paying for this?"

"Davey is. In fact, it was his idea."

"Like hell it was."

"If you don't believe me, ask him."

I plan on it, though this is not what I say. "I am running a business here. I do not have room in my schedule for your whims."

"We'll see about that."

I watch as she starts toward the front of the house. She almost reaches the door before she stops and turns on her heel. "Oh," she says like she's forgotten one tiny detail. "What should we do about Cole?"

"What about him?"

"Think we should invite him, too? Considering?"

"Considering what?"

"Don't be dense, Ruth. That man is head over heels in love with you. It would be a real shame for him to get hurt."

CHAPTER TWENTY-THREE

Ruth

My mouth is open but I cannot force sound out of it. I try to call out for help, but a lump has formed in my throat and I cannot seem to form words around it. What comes out is raspy and hoarse. I sound like a dying animal.

Oh my God. Oh my God. Oh my God.

Please, no. Please. Please don't let this be happening.

My tongue feels like it weighs a hundred pounds. It sticks to the roof of my mouth like sandpaper. I take the steps two or three at a time, going just as fast as I can manage until I reach the last one.

Julia is lying at the bottom of the stairs, her eyes fixed on the ceiling. She isn't moving. I'm not even sure she is breathing.

"Help!" I yell, willing someone to appear. "Hello?" I call out, hoping someone will hear me, hoping someone will come. "I need help! Now!"

No one answers. No one comes.

I have no idea where Johnny or Davis are or where Ashley or whatever the hell her name happens to be is. I only know that I'm calling for help and that it seems I'm on my own.

Kneeling beside Julia, I plead loudly, very loudly, for her not to be dead. My fingers find her neck and then her wrist and everything happens in slow motion as I check her pulse. Do I feel something? A faint rhythm beating against the pads of my fingers? I can't tell.

I lay my head on her chest and listen for the familiar drum of a heartbeat. It's hard to hear anything over the sound of my panicked breath. This doesn't make any sense. I was just laughing with her. *What was it? Twenty minutes ago?*

Smoothing her hair, I tell her she is going to be okay, even though I'm not sure it's true. I call out again, several times, but when no one comes, I realize I have to leave her and get help myself. I dart to the kitchen where I yank the receiver off the old corded phone attached to the wall. I dial 9-1-1 and then I stretch the cord as far as it will go, so that I round the corner just enough so that I can see her. I don't know why this matters, only that I'm panicking, and that it does.

As I wait for the dispatcher to pick up, I'm pretty sure I hear movement coming from upstairs. Footsteps or some sort of shuffling. Hairs stand on the back of my neck. I sense someone watching me, but when I look around, no one is there. Then, there's more shuffling. It's lighter this time. It could be a guest or it could be an ax murderer. Nothing in this house feels normal anymore. Friend or foe, surely whoever is up there would have come when they heard me screaming for help. *Unless...*

I give the dispatcher our address. I request an ambulance. Then I lay the phone down, leaving it dangling from the cord. Our insurance company made me take a training class once in exchange for a discount on our policy. They taught me a lot of things, one of them being that in the event of an emergency or an accident on the premises, to say as little as possible. Nothing other than pertinent medical information should be conveyed without an attorney present.

The ambulance arrives within four minutes. I listen to the paramedics as they work. They suspect cardiac arrest. Julia's breathing is shallow. She has a pulse. She is not dead. But she does not regain consciousness. As the paramedics wheel her out on a stretcher, and I am questioned, it occurs to me that I am going to have to call her family. I don't want to have to be the one, but who else is there?

As they load her in the ambulance, I stand at the curb holding her rosary beads. The man who lives next door comes over to ask if there's anything he can do to help. When I tell him there isn't, he says, "I hope you have good worker's comp."

It feels like such an odd thing to say, but then I realize that I don't know what our insurance coverage is, and anyway, that's the last thing I should be thinking about at a time like this.

But he goes on. "I see this all the time. People trying to get out of a hard day's work."

"Excuse me?"

"Oh." He shifts on his feet and extends his hand. "I'm sorry. How rude of me. I've forgotten to introduce myself, I'm Zach."

"Ruth."

"Yes," he smiles. "Lily told me all about you."

The police briefly speak to the paramedics. I try to make out what they are saying, but the man, Zach, he won't stop talking. "You wouldn't believe the things people do. Anything to keep from getting their hands dirty."

I want to throat punch him. He doesn't know it, but he is literally talking about a woman who is a second mother to me. I lost the first one, and while it seems preposterous now, it never occurred to me that this one wouldn't live forever.

CHAPTER TWENTY-FOUR

Passerby

A gentle shove down the stairs was all it took. It wasn't my proudest moment, but sometimes you gotta do what you gotta do. I don't usually go around taking down old ladies, but this one had it coming to her. And really, she was going to die before too long anyway, so why not save her the trouble of losing her looks, her hearing, and her mind beforehand. You wouldn't let fruit sit and rot away on your kitchen counter. Why let a human go through that experience?

Wouldn't it be better to go out on a good day doing what you love?

Except, and this is my one regret, it wasn't a good day for her doing what she loved. It was just like every other day: her cleaning up after other people, her taking care of other people's messes and doing it all with a fake smile plastered on her face. Tell me, what kind of person would want an existence like that?

So, you see, time was of the essence. She should have kept her mouth shut. What is it with people in this day and age that they simply cannot mind their own business? Let it be known: meddling only leads to trouble and in the end that's exactly what she got.

CHAPTER TWENTY-FIVE

Ruth

"She is not who you think she is," I say to Davis after storming the guest house. Thankfully, he's alone. I have just spoken with Julia's family at the hospital, and it was the third worst thing I've ever had to do.

"Where is she, anyway?"

He looks up from his laptop. "She went into town."

"Perfect." She seems to go into town a lot now that Davis has gotten her a rental car. "Because we need to talk."

"Good evening to you, too."

He says this to annoy me. We are not, nor have we ever been, the type of family to cower or to hide behind small talk. "It's not a good evening. You could be over at the house helping out. Then it might be a good evening."

"You're in such a great mood, I'm just dying to be around you."

"Half of that statement just might be true."

He turns his attention back to his computer, and he tilts his chin in my direction. He doesn't look at me, though. "What is it Ruth? What can I do for you?"

I smile. I'm really glad he asked. "You know what I find interesting?"

"No. But I'm certain you're going to tell me."

"Ashley—or is it Caitlyn?"

"It's Ashley."

"You sure about that?"

He looks at me then. "Are *you* sure?"

"I'm not sure of anything when it comes to her."

"Get to the point, would you? I haven't got all night."

"What are you doing?" I ask this because I'm curious, but also, I have a right to know. Davis doesn't really work. He's what you might call a "dabbler." He tries things, but he never sticks with them. Certainly not long enough to make any money, anyway. Mostly, he lives off distributions from the trust that our parents left for us. It's a sore subject between the three of us, seeing that Johnny and I, we actually work for a living.

"Research. I'm thinking about getting into investing."

This sounds like a terrible idea, but right now I'm trying to pick my battles, and it's one of his other whims that I'm more concerned about at the moment.

"Ashley—she doesn't seem to be the least bit worried about getting shot up and run off the road. Doesn't that seem a little strange to you?"

"Not everyone lives their life in fear, Ruth. Not everyone is you."

"Just explain to me what you're thinking with her. I have to know."

"My relationship is none of your business."

"Bullshit!" I feel heat creeping up on my cheeks like a hot summer's day. Any prior notion I had of remaining calm flies right out the window. "You made it my business by bringing her here!"

"This is my house too."

"So?"

"So," he repeats in a sing-song voice, mocking me like we're children again.

"She lied about something as basic as her name. What else do you think she's lying about?"

"Lots of people go by names that aren't theirs. It's a nickname." He shakes his head slowly from side to side and then meets my eye. "Why do you care so much, anyway? You're not the one marrying her."

"You don't even know anything about her."

"How do you know what I know?"

I want to drop-kick him. He sounds like such an entitled brat. Come to think of it, he always has been. "Do you know where she went to college? *If* she went to college? Do you know that she's not actually a teacher?"

He laughs angrily. "You're so sure of yourself, Ruth."

"And you're avoiding the question."

"I'm not avoiding it. It's just that I don't owe you an answer. In fact, I don't owe you anything."

"You're engaged to someone you don't even know, Davis." I sigh heavily. "What the fuck?"

"I have nothing more to say to you, Ruth." His tone is dripping with venom. "I'm not defending—I'm not *discussing* my life choices with you. Anything to do with me and my future wife—it doesn't concern you."

"Why are you in such a rush to get married? I don't get it. What's wrong with dating? Maybe live together for longer than five seconds. You just met and suddenly you're ready to make a lifelong commitment."

He gives me a look and suddenly something snaps into place and a lot of thoughts come through at once. It's like a download from the universe. And then, in that instant, I get it. Finally an answer that makes sense. "Wait a minute…"

"Ruth. Stop." My brother knows me well enough to know where this is going. He can see it in my eyes. I'm on to him.

"Not only do you not know her, you haven't even had sex with her."

I'm half-expecting him to deny it. But when I see his expression, and the way he sets his shoulders, I know he can't. "Not everyone has loose morals, Ruth."

"Oh, my God." I throw up my hands. "You are so fucking stupid."

CHAPTER TWENTY-SIX

Ruth

After my conversation with Davis, not much happens. The days pass in a hazy blur. They all seem to fold in on one another, blending together, until it truly feels like it might actually be an endless summer.

With Julia in the hospital, things around Magnolia House are particularly hectic but also quiet in a way that makes me sad. She's always been like my right arm, and the more time that passes without her, the harder time I have managing. While I haven't quite figured out Ashley's con, I do at least have a sense of the game she's playing, and my initial enthusiasm for figuring out her motives starts to fizzle.

If Davis wants to be an idiot, he deserves what he gets. That's what Johnny said. If only I could get fully on board with that sentiment.

Even so, the fight drains out of me some. I revert back to not wanting to get out of bed. I don't feel like working. I don't feel like doing much of anything. The days drag and the nights seem to expand out forever. Grief settles deep and heavy in my bones. It feels like the fog will never lift, that it may never leave. There are some days I cannot sleep and some days that's all I want to do— some days it's all I *can* do.

I hire a temp from the small agency in town. She picks up some of the slack. Johnny helps with the rest, although I do my best not to let my mood affect my work. And when I can't help it, tequila helps me get through the day.

Then the letter comes. Like a lot of things in my life recently, it arrives out of nowhere. I can't say that I am not expecting it. But I can't say that I am, either.

I have a hard time making sense of it. First, I'm sad. And then I'm angry. And after that, I'm just bitter. The lows are low, and sometimes I manage hope, but it feels too sporadic, too short-lived to count for much.

I guess what I'm trying to say is Julia has worked for my family for over forty years. Since she was a teenager. Since long before I was born. She changed my diapers and carried me and my brothers around on her hip. On the rare occurrence that my parents left town, she stayed with us.

If my memory serves me correctly, they only went out of town twice, once to see a specialist, and the other time for a funeral. They hated to leave Magnolia House just as much as they hated leaving us. It was their baby in the same way that we were, and they saw little point in being anywhere but here. The fact that they left things in Julia's hands says it all. It wasn't like they didn't have family here. It was that they trusted Julia more than anyone.

When the constable appears on the porch, I am not expecting what happens next. For several long moments, I stare at him through the screen door. I'm expecting him to tell me he's come to arrest Davis, and I'm contemplating places to hide him, the best way to get him out of town, or out of the country if it comes to that. It feels like a ticking time bomb, my brother's freedom.

Between Bobby Holt and Danny Vera, it seems like he's bound to be accused of something. Whatever that something is, I just hope it isn't murder.

"I'm looking for Ruth Channing," the officer says, after tipping his hat. His tone tells me he's all business. His demeanor tells me he's polite.

"You're looking at her."

He hands me the manila envelope. He does not tell me I've been served. But that's exactly what has happened.

CHAPTER TWENTY-SEVEN

Ruth

"She's not even dead," Cole says. My head is on his chest and I'm naked in his bed, and it's as though I haven't made enough mistakes lately, I had to go and make one more. I don't care. I needed something to break me out of my funk, and it seemed like an orgasm would surely do it. Plus, I needed a little honesty, even if it's soft, and I'm not sure I believe it. It feels good. Momentarily, at least.

"I know. But they want us to cover her medical bills. They're mounting up. I can imagine it's a lot for them. Nevertheless, I didn't think they'd sue."

"What did you think would happen?"

"I figured they'd work it out with our insurance company," I sigh. "I don't know what I thought. But I really didn't think they'd make it this personal."

"It's not personal."

"Well, it feels that way."

"I wouldn't worry too much. She'll wake up soon, and this will all be a distant memory."

I lift my head and search his eyes. "And if she doesn't?"

"She will. Julia would never sue your family. She *is* family."

"That means nothing."

"True," he smiles. "I don't know, Ruth. What do you want me to say?"

"I could lose everything."

"You will never lose everything."

"Davis suggested we sell."

Cole's brow rises.

"I know. And he's the one who's always on my side. He's the one who keeps Johnny at bay."

"I haven't heard Johnny mention selling—not in a while."

"He has. Here and there. He gets tired of hearing me complain." I lay my head on his chest once again, this time scooting in closer. "He doesn't understand. It comes with the territory. I mean… He complains about the fire department all the time. But dare anyone suggest *he* quit?"

"What are you gonna do?"

"I don't know." Cole pulls the sheet up and tucks it around me. "Strange things have been happening. Things I can't explain."

"Like?"

"Weird noises. And I get the feeling that someone's watching me. A lot."

"Hmmm."

"It's her fault," I say. "This is all her fault." I recant the conversation between me and Ashley the other day in the parlor. Cole is riveted through it all. I know because I make sure to watch his face as I tell the story. "See?" I say when I'm done. "She's crazy."

"She's young."

"Young and crazy. Not a good combo."

I watch as he lifts the covers and climbs out of bed. "It'll all shake out, one way or another."

"That's not very comforting."

"What would make you feel better?"

"Get back in bed. I'll show you."

Cole gives me a wide-eyed look. "I'm going to need a minute."

"Fine." I shrug. "Then tell me the truth. What do you really think?"

"All right." He looks around the room and then runs his fingers through his hair. "The truth."

I wait for what feels like a very long time until finally he looks back at me. "You know, Ruth, people that fuck with other people's hearts tend to get what's coming to them."

I don't know if he's referring to Ashley Parker or to me or perhaps even to himself. I don't even know if I agree. I only know I don't want to argue. Sex this good isn't easy to come by. "Wait. Where are you going?"

"To the kitchen," he says, pulling on his boxers. "Want anything?"

"No, I can't stay."

He turns and looks over his shoulder, brows raised toward the ceiling. "When have you ever?"

"I have," I say, and I try to recall a time, but I can't. Running a bed and breakfast doesn't really afford me the kind of lifestyle of not being around to see that said breakfast is prepared.

"You're welcome to stay. You know that. But I'm not going to beg."

He makes me smile. He had no problem with it just a few minutes ago. "Please?"

Cole picks up my T-shirt and throws it at me. "Never."

"A lot can happen between now and never."

We don't talk about what happened before. I can't call it a fight, because it wasn't that. It never is. We just walk out of each other's lives until one of us gets needy or desperate or both and somehow finds our way back in. And then it's like nothing happened, though of course it did. You can bury quite a lot with good sex and decent conversation.

"You coming? I bought ice cream yesterday. Rocky Road."

I roll my eyes behind his back. Rocky Road is my favorite, and he knows this, which means his purchase was either wishful thinking or deep knowing and both scare me a little.

I don't bother putting my T-shirt or anything else on when I follow him to the kitchen. I need him to want me to come back. And part of me somewhere deep down wants him to ask me again to stay. That part of me, the weak part, it wants him to keep asking until I do.

As he pulls two bowls from the open cupboard, I glance around the kitchen. Two wine glasses sit next to the sink. I do not miss the lipstick stain on one of them. It's been a long time since I've worn makeup. He sets the bowls down and walks over to the freezer.

I hop up on his counter. "I feel like I need to make my move."

He fills a glass with water and hands it to me. "Your move? What's your move?"

I'm talking about the situation with the lawsuit, mostly. But I'm talking about a lot of things. "I don't know. I'm still deciding."

"Just be careful what hill you pick to defend. You may die doing it."

I'm afraid he's more accurate than he realizes.

"Instead of ice cream, can I have a drink?"

He pulls open his liquor cabinet and motions. "Pick your poison."

"Tequila."

I watch as he fills a tumbler. "You aren't drinking with me tonight?"

He shrugs. "Might as well."

Cole puts on an old record and we sit on his porch drinking and talking for a long time. I want to ask about the wine glass, but I don't. It's peaceful out here, and I'd like to keep it that way.

"She's like the Trojan horse, Ashley is. But I think maybe there are bigger fish to fry. At least for the time being. I'm not going to just sit here and let them take my house. What's next after that? Where does it stop? Where does it end?"

"Who, the court?" Cole cocks his head. "Julia's family?"

"Anyone."

"They can't make you sell your house, Ruth. But they can make things pretty rough for you."

"What should I do?"

He finishes off his glass, places it on the arm of his chair, and looks over at me. "I haven't the faintest idea."

I watch him pick up the bottle and refill his glass. He starts to fill mine too, but I wave him away. "I have to get going soon."

"You asked me what you should do."

"Yeah."

"Do you want to know what I really think?"

"I wouldn't have asked if I didn't."

"I think you should marry me."

I laugh, and then he laughs, even though nothing is really funny. We don't look at each other or speak much after that. And that's my signal that it's time to leave.

CHAPTER TWENTY-EIGHT

Ruth

There are eight miles from Cole's cabin to Magnolia House. For six of them I am followed. It's either a pickup truck or an SUV tailing me, I'm not sure which. I call Cole first, considering he's the closest.

There aren't many vehicles on the road this time of night, especially not way out here. So when the driver comes on my tail fast and doesn't pass, I know something isn't right. He flips on his brights and rides my bumper. Ordinarily, I'd move to the side and let him pass, but on a two-lane country road in the middle of nowhere at this hour, he has options. He can go around.

Only he doesn't go around. He pulls up close and taps my fender with the front of his truck. It's a dangerous maneuver, especially at this speed, and I am certain I am going to die. I reach into my purse and fish for my pistol, only to find it isn't there. I keep a spare in the glove box, but I can't reach it from the driver's seat without leaning way over.

"Drive to the police station," Cole says through the speaker. "He won't follow you there."

"Okay." I am just hoping I don't die before then. "How far away are you?"

"Not far, I don't think."

"Cole?" I scream. "He's bumping me. I'm going to lose control, or he's going to run me off the road."

"Stay calm. I'm not far." He speaks slowly, drawing his words out. I realize how much he had to drink, and I instantly regret calling. "Can you give a description of the vehicle?"

"It's dark. I can't see anything. Not with his bright lights in my eyes."

"It's the Holts," he says, although it feels like he's speaking more to himself than to me. "I'd put good money on it. They've gone awfully quiet since Bobby died. And for them, that's never a good sign."

"Please hurry."

"I'm coming up behind you now."

Seeing another set of headlights allows me a sigh of relief, but just a small one. That's when I hear it. Loud popping sounds. I hear the engine behind me rev and then there are headlights coming around me and up beside me. A vehicle passes doing at least a hundred and when I look in my rearview mirror, there's only darkness.

CHAPTER TWENTY-NINE

Ruth

I 'll give anything. I'll do anything. Just let him be alive. Without even thinking, I slam on the brakes quickly, bringing my car to a full stop. I throw it into park, push the door open, and take off in a full sprint toward Cole's truck. A nearly full moon lights the sky, but still it's dark and I can hardly see where I'm running to. But I am not thinking. At least not rationally. I am running, and I have only one goal. That's getting to him and making sure he's alive.

His truck is partially in a ditch, which makes it hard to see from the road, unless you're looking. His tail lights are lit, which helps. I use the flashlight on my phone to guide me down the embankment.

I pray the short way down. *Let him be okay.*

When I reach the truck, I try to open the driver's door. It won't budge, so I try to go in through the passenger side and I realize they're both locked. I search the ground and then the bed of his truck, looking for something to break a window. I can see Cole inside, slumped over the steering wheel. I beat on the window with my fists.

The heavy scent of gasoline fills the air.

I work up the courage to break the glass with my hand. Pulling off my T-shirt, I wrap it around my arm as many times as I can manage. Briefly, I consider running back to my car, but I worry that the truck will go up in flames in the meantime. He would burn alive, and I would never forgive myself.

Thankfully, I don't have to make that choice because I hear sirens in the distance, and within seconds state troopers are on the scene.

I watch helplessly as they break the glass and pull Cole from the truck. They lay him out on the pavement.

An officer pulls me back and peppers me with questions, and I am so sick of this. I only want to make sure Cole is okay, and maybe that makes me combative and uncooperative. But I'm sick of ambulances and hospitals and seeing people I care about require medical attention.

Eventually, Cole regains consciousness. I answer their questions and calm down enough that they allow me to ride with him in the ambulance. He doesn't remember anything prior to the crash. He can't recall why he was on the road, or what he was doing, or even whether he was following a truck. He doesn't remember me calling.

I tell the officer about being followed. About being rammed from behind. I explain I know it was a Ford by the emblem on the grill. I know it was a dark truck with a crew cab, and that I suspect it being one of the Holts', but I do not know what they drive because I've never paid much attention.

They ask me to do a sobriety test.

They tell me Cole failed his. His blood alcohol level is two-

and-a-half times the legal limit. He has a concussion and cervical sprains.

And I may have just ruined his life.

CHAPTER THIRTY

Passerby

Some people. They just don't know when enough is enough. It's the greatest travesty, really. When a good person sticks their nose where it doesn't belong. When they don't know when to leave well enough alone.

It happens. I get it. We've all been there.

I may or may not be there now.

It's just... In that case, you have to do something about it.

I should have killed him. Even if that wasn't really my intention, I should have. There's no room in this world for being soft. When something gets in your way, when it stands between you and what you want, well, only one person can win. We're not all winners, and there's no trophy for participation, no matter what people want you to believe. You either win or you don't, and that is that.

For me, there's still time to settle the score. Even though I've gone about it the hard way.

I don't often make mistakes but when I do...well...

It's always the things you leave undone that come back to bite you in the ass.

CHAPTER THIRTY-ONE

Ruth

I am not expecting to find both of my brothers *and* Ashley in the kitchen when I get home from the hospital. I come in the back door hoping to avoid guests, but also my family, only to find them seated at the table.

Despite doing my best to act nonchalant about the fact that all eyes are on me, my hands shake. The way they're looking at me, it isn't good. They know what I've done. They sense my guilt. The pity written on their faces tells me they're not all up at this hour out of coincidence. They're waiting on me.

I know instantly, something is wrong.

"How's Cole?" Johnny asks.

"He's okay," I say, dropping my purse onto the table. "Not great. But he's home at least."

I walk over to the coffee pot, pull a mug from the cabinet, and pour a cup. "Those state troopers..." My eyes meet Johnny's.

"They're relentless. They were going to send a man with a head injury to the slammer."

Everyone looks at me, but I'm not sure if it's out of surprise or concern. I press my lips to the cup and feel thankful for its warmth. The rest of the kitchen is filled with icy stares. "Had to get some strings pulled," I add. "Thank God for favors."

"I'm just glad he's alive," Johnny says.

Resting the small of my back against the counter, I shift in his direction. "I'm surprised you weren't there."

"I was on call. I couldn't leave the station. Not till about a half-hour ago. And by that point, I heard he was headed home."

"I see." I glance from Johnny to Davis and back. "I take it y'all aren't gathered here for chit-chat. So, what is it?"

Johnny shifts in his chair. "Julia passed away last night."

His words hit me like a sucker punch. I expected something, but it wasn't that. I try to form a response, only nothing worth saying comes to mind. I grip the coffee mug so tight I'm afraid it might break into a million tiny pieces. Bile rises in my throat. I think I might be sick.

"Ashley went to see her last night, at least."

"Why would she do that?" I say, just before I turn and look at her directly. "Why would you do that?"

"Ruth," Davis warns. "Don't start—"

"What?" I scoff. "I can't ask the question? Mike advised us to stay away. On account of the lawsuit. Her going there was out of line. She didn't even know Julia!"

"I knew her," Ashley says. "Not as well as you guys but—"

"Shut up. I don't care." There's more I want to say. A lot more. Only I'm too enraged, and suddenly I feel very, very tired. The lack of sleep combined with everything that's happened just hits me like a freight train. I should have been there. *I* should have gone to see her. But when our family attorney advised against it, when he said that doing so could only make things worse, that I could lose everything, I listened. Now, I realize what a mistake that was. A mistake that can't be undone.

"Her family wasn't even there," Ashley says, incredulously.

I dump the coffee in the sink and toss the mug in with it. The noise startles everyone. "I'm going to bed."

"Wait," Davis says. "We want to talk to you. And not just about Julia."

"Not about Julia alone," Ashley corrects him.

"We think you need a break." Davis tells me. He speaks slowly and calmly. Davis does not sound like himself. He doesn't sound like anyone I know.

"Why don't you take a trip?" Johnny says, and it's not really a question. He makes that much clear with his sharp tone. "This house is taking its toll on you."

"It makes sense *you* would say that, seeing as you're just dying to sell it out from under me."

"I'm not the bad guy, Ruth." Johnny looks down at the table. "When's the last time you took a day off?"

"People around town are starting to talk," Davis says.

"How is that anything new? That's all anyone around here ever does. They talk. And nothing changes. It's called living in a small town. It's a fishbowl."

"A vacation might do you good," Ashley says. "I know it has me. You never know. Getting out of the fishbowl could be cleansing for the soul."

I glare at her for a quick beat. "Go fuck yourself."

Both Johnny and Davis shake their heads. I know it isn't exactly lady like to speak that way. I've tasted enough soap in my lifetime to know. People in this town gossip about my outbursts. But I don't care. This woman walks into my house, walks in from nowhere, and thinks she knows what's best for me. That's cute.

"Don't be rude," Davis says. "Ashley's just trying to help."

"I said what I said. I have zero remorse."

My gaze flits between Davis and Johnny. "And who came up with this grand idea, anyway? *Her?* It couldn't have been you two, that's for sure. It's not like you're going to step up to the plate and take care of things around here. Obviously, this place doesn't just run itself. But you wouldn't know that, given either of you hardly lift a finger."

Johnny folds his hands and places them on the table. It looks like he's praying and it reminds me of so many dinners we've had in years past. "We could always put selling back on the table."

I sensed this coming, but that doesn't mean it stings any less. They've been bringing the subject up more and more lately.

"Ashley thinks she might have found a buyer," Davis says.

"Fuck Ashley. And fuck her buyer."

"I won't allow you to speak to my fiancée that way, Ruth."

"Well then, fuck you, too." Then, I turn to her. "You know, it's funny. Everything you touch in this town ends up dead or worse."

She looks at me and swallows hard. "What's worse than dead?"

"If you're not careful you might just find out."

"Ruth, don't threaten people. Ashley is a guest. Could you try to maybe be a little less offensive?" Johnny says. He seems almost serious. But I can tell he's mocking the situation. My older brother always has loved a good cat fight. Even better if he's the source. I can also tell that he's envious of Davis, and that is doing me no favors.

"Is that what she is?" I ask. "A guest? No, it can't be."

Davis pushes away from the table.

"Because guests—" I say. "They pay their way. They bring something to the table. *Her,* she's done nothing *but* cause trouble. And"—I motion around the kitchen— "all on the trust's dime."

"See?" She looks at Davis. "This is what I'm talking about. She's abusive."

"Ashley is right. We've planned sort of an intervention here," Davis says. "I don't think you should make things worse for yourself."

I walk over to the door and hold it open. "Get out."

"Ruth," Johnny and Davis say at the same time. "Calm down."

"Don't tell me to calm down!"

"This," Ashley says, tossing up her hands. "*This* is what I'm talking about."

The three of them study me curiously, like I'm on exhibit at the local zoo, like some kind of animal, and they're both interested and terrified of what I might do.

"She told us what happened," Davis informs me.

My brow furrows because there's no telling what she said. It could literally be anything.

Ashley rolls one sleeve on her pajama top and pushes it above her elbow.

Davis sighs sorrowfully. "She showed us the scratches on her arms."

"You attacked me," she says. "I mean... I know you were upset, but it's no excuse. Violence is never an excuse."

My eyes widen, and a lump the size of a grapefruit forms in my throat. I've seen a lot of things. Nothing like this. "She's lying."

"You got my best friend arrested," Johnny tells me. "Not to mention, almost killed."

"First of all, someone was following me. They were ramming my car. *I* could have been killed. Cole showing up very well might've saved my life."

"I don't know, Ruth..." Davis chimes in. "Don't you think it's possible you're overreacting?"

"What? You mean like last time? When my car got shot up?"

"This seems different."

"Different how?"

Davis raises his brow. "My guess? It was probably just kids messing with you. Teenagers with nothing better to do..."

"Right," I say with an eye roll. "And I've got oceanfront property in Arizona."

Then I turn to Johnny. "And about Cole—if you cared about either of us, you would have shown up."

"I was at work."

"You're literally a first responder."

"You can't expect someone to always come to your rescue, Ruth. It's not like it would've made any difference. The damage was already done. It *has* been done for a long time."

Davis and Johnny and Ashley, they're coming at me from all sides. I'm running out of fight, so I turn away. I need a second to think. Outside, the sun is starting to peek through the trees. Already, the steady drone of a lawn mower hums in the distance. The sound reminds me of something, something I hadn't thought of. "I can't leave now."

They all wait for me to say whatever it is I'm going to say next. I stall for maximum effect. "If I left now, I'd miss the engagement party."

"But after," Davis replies, his tone hopeful. "You'll go somewhere after? Just a little vacation."

"Sure, why not." I shrug. "A road trip sounds fun."

"Good," Ashley says, rubbing her forearm. "You really need it."

I flip on the faucet and glance over my shoulder. "And who knows? Maybe I'll even come home with a new fiancé."

CHAPTER THIRTY-TWO

Ruth

There's good news and there's bad news. And some middle of the road kind in between. The way I see it, I have a few options. There's a lot up in the air. But the good news is, I have a deep sense of knowing what it is I have to do.

The first thing: after I make sure breakfast is handled for guests, I need to catch a few hours of sleep.

This is the easy part. I set my alarm, close my eyes, and fall into a fitful sleep. When my alarm goes off a little before noon, I wake with cotton mouth and a foggy mind.

A cold shower helps, and afterward, I feel like a million bucks. At least, this is what I tell myself, anyway. Mind over matter.

Forty-eight hours is all that stands between now and the engagement party. This means I have a lot to do in a short amount of time.

Second thing, I call Roy. I need his help. Not only with the situation with Cole. But there's something else, something I hadn't thought of. I ask him to stop by because I know it'll be easier in person.

While I'm waiting for him to arrive, I keep myself busy by doing some digging. It's stormy out, which fits my mood. I try Cole.

Gina answers his phone. And nothing surprises me anymore. He's pissed at me, and this is his way of passively aggressively showing me. He recalls last night very differently than I do. In his mind, we had a fight, the usual one, about commitment. He was drunk, so he remembers things a little differently. In his mind, I took off, and he followed. The details of how and why he ended up on that farm to market road are rather hazy.

I've been a friend of the bottle myself. So, I suppose I understand, even though I don't. Not really. I guess we all run out of good favor sometime. Still, it hurts that Cole would turn his back on me. That he would blame me. He could have been the hero, but instead, he's taking the victim route. It doesn't make any sense. But then, his hangover hasn't even had time to wear off fully. Anything can still happen.

The situation with Cole bothers me enough that it motivates me to become a keyboard warrior. After all, the rage has to go somewhere.

Finally, it seems to pay off when I find a forum online that mentions the name Caitlyn Jepson. When I click on the thumbnail, I am not expecting much. I do not actually believe that the name on the driver's license—Caitlyn Jepson — is anymore her real name than Ashley is.

Jackpot. The image loads and chills creep up my spine. It's a picture of Ashley a.k.a Caitlyn, only with darker hair. She looks a little younger in the photo, which could be a result of the hair color, although the photo can't be *that* old. Because whoever she is, the woman my brother is engaged to, Ashley—she isn't that old.

The OP as many of the comments reference, or the original

poster "Chris" writes: Beware if you see this woman. She stole from me. She's a scam artist. DM for more info.

Within ninety seconds, I've created an account, clicked on his username, and hit send on a direct message. I keep it short and simple. *I think a friend might be involved with this woman. Would you be willing to chat?*

Two hours go by. I check my inbox at least a dozen times. Nothing. The post was written six months ago, so who knows. People write a lot of things on the internet in the heat of the moment. Maybe he's put the situation behind him. Maybe he has no intention of digging up the past.

I'M SITTING IN ONE OF THE WINGBACK CHAIRS IN THE LIBRARY, WITH my laptop teetering on my lap when Ashley comes strolling in. Davis follows at her heel, which I'm grateful for. I don't want to be alone with her.

I don't trust her. But more than that, I don't trust myself.

It's also a double-edged sword. I need to talk to her alone. Risky as that may be.

The worst of the storm has passed but the rain remains.

"There you are," Davis says. His hair is windblown and he's soaked from head to toe. But my attention is on Ashley. She's beaming. She's grinning from ear to ear and she looks absolutely radiant, even wet. I've seen this same twinkle in the eyes of brides-to-be many, many times. It's the look of someone getting everything they've ever wanted. I didn't think it was possible to hate her anymore, but sometimes I surprise even myself. "We've just been in town finalizing the floral arrangements for Saturday night," Davis tells me. "Wait till you see them. Mrs. Adkins has really outdone herself."

My brow furrows. "Since when do you care about flowers?"

"He doesn't," Ashley quips. "Afterward we dropped by the caterers to taste test the menu."

"It was the food for me," he confesses.

"But that's not all," Ashley says. She gives my brother the side eye. "Do you want to tell her? Or should I?"

"It's your news. You tell her."

Ashley claps her hands giddily and then rubs her palms together. "I'm starting a business!"

Davis nods. "Ashley is incredible. She's already landed three clients."

My lips press into a tight smile. I should have seen this coming. She is never going to leave.

"Tell her," Davis urges.

"Well, after spending so much time in town, I realized how much easier it would be if I had the option to search online before spending the time to drive in."

"Such hard work shopping is."

"Right?" Her eyes widen. She feels happy to be understood. "That and with all the tourists, if they had an online presence, I have no doubt they'd get a lot of repeat business."

I almost laugh. Thankfully, I mange to refrain. The joke is on her and I can't wait to get to the punchline. Residents of Jester Falls are *people*, people. They aren't tech savvy. They're relationship savvy.

"Ashley is helping Georgia Adkins and Ms. Anita get set up online."

She nods. "I think with them on board, I can get the rest of the town behind the idea. It could really do a lot for the local economy."

A notification flashes across my laptop screen. I agree. "It's amazing the things you can find online."

Ashley grins proudly, the way people do when they think they've won.

"You see," Davis says, nudging her with his elbow. "I told you my sister could be nice when she wants to be."

He glares at me, and then he places his hand on the small of Ashley's back. "It just takes her a little time to warm up is all."

I watch as he leads her out of the room.

Ashley turns and glances over her shoulder. Behind her back she tosses up her middle finger. I don't even care. Chris from the internet has just messaged me back.

CHAPTER THIRTY-THREE

Ruth

It takes several hours, but Roy does finally show up. The storms left downed trees and debris strewn about, which left several residents stranded. Needless to say, when he arrives he isn't in the best mood, but most things can be fixed, and thankfully Roy is one of them.

He leans against his cruiser, his arms folded across his chest. He waits for me to come to him, which is an interesting maneuver on his part. Roy is aware he has something I need, and he has decided he isn't going to make it easy.

I offer a friendly wave from the porch. I will make myself small for him, because the situation calls for it, and ultimately that's what he wants.

Roy has always reminded me, and the rest of the town, of Barney Fife from The Andy Griffith show. We used to call him that growing up, and sometimes I wonder if he actually wanted to be a police officer, or if everyone's teasing sent him on that track.

I don't know what makes me think of those days, of taunting him on the playground. Maybe it's seeing him here, knowing that he has the upper hand and wondering if perhaps he always did. I guess you don't know what you don't know. Certainly, no one is teasing him now, and no one below the age of thirty has any recollection of that show, something I think Roy is grateful for.

"You called?" he says, as I reach the edge of the drive. I stop there, with my hands on my hips like there's an invisible line drawn in the sand. He looks at me with thinly veiled disdain. "I take it this has something to do with last night?"

I have to admit, I have a lot on my mind. It had not occurred to me that Roy would be angry with me about the situation with Cole. But he is, and the storms and downed trees have nothing on that anger.

"No," I say. "Actually it doesn't."

"What can I do for you, Ruth?"

I look away. "There's someone out there... someone who wants me dead. And I think I might know who it is."

His expression tells me he thinks I'm being dramatic. "Who's that?"

"I don't want to name names. I mean... I shouldn't. Not unless I'm sure. Right?"

"Well, the way I see it..." His gaze follows mine. "You can start naming names or you could wait until it's too late. It's your call."

"I know you're angry with me," I say, because sometimes it's better to call out the proverbial elephant in the room straight-away. "And you have a right to be."

"You have terrible taste in men."

Our eyes meet. "I've seen worse."

"You used to be different."

"Maybe you just didn't know me."

"Impossible."

It's not. When Roy looks at me, he sees what he wants to see. "You think?"

"It doesn't matter what I think." He looks away. "Why'd you call?"

"I was wondering if you might arrest Davis."

"For what?"

I'm trying to be funny, but he's not taking the bait. There were two ways this could go, and luckily for my brother, the internet came through. That's not to say I am above having him put in jail; anything to save him and our business from that woman. Still, that would be a low blow. Even for me. "To keep him from marrying that woman."

"Apparently not even the prospect of jail can keep true love away. But you know that, don't you, Ruth?"

"I do. But I know something else."

"Pray tell."

"I know fresh starts are possible."

"Bless your heart," he tells me, which in the south sounds a whole lot like *fuck you*. "I've been in this business a long time…"

I don't know what business he's talking about, but I know that I'm about to find out. "People don't really change."

"They can't," I say. "Not if you refuse them the chance. Which is why I called—" I flash a devilish grin. "I need a date for Saturday night."

Roy looks at me in disbelief. He narrows his eyes. I don't know if there's hope hidden in those eyes, only that I need there to be. I think for his sake, he does too. "What's the catch?"

"There's no catch."

"Let me guess. You want me to make Cole Wheeler jealous."

"Of course not. Jesus, Roy. I'm not that petty."

"Who then? Ryan?"

"It hurts that you think so little of me."

"It's a terrible plan, Ruth. And it won't work."

"I should hope not." I get the sense he wants me to say more. More than anything, he wants to be right. He wants me to give just a little, and so I do. "And why is that? Why won't it work?"

"It just won't." He crosses and uncrosses his arms, only to cross them again. "Cole nor Ryan will ever believe, not anymore than I do, that you're interested in me."

He shifts his stance. "And even if they did—your penchant for unavailable men will do you no favors in the long run."

"Well, it's a good thing that wasn't at all what I had in mind." I say this and then I do the opposite of what he expects me to do: I do not argue with him. I lean forward and I kiss him full on the mouth and I don't let him pull away, not even when he tries. "You see, Roy, I don't give a fuck what anyone thinks. I want what I want."

He looks rattled. "And what's that?"

"I told you. For you to be my date at my brother's engagement party."

"What else?"

"I want you to pull all you can on the name Caitlyn Jepson."

"That would be breaking the rules."

"Yes," I say. "But I promise I would make it worth your while."

He tips his hat and opens the driver's door of his squad car. After he climbs in and closes it, he looks at me. "I'm sure you would."

"I hope you won't let me down, Roy," I say, leaning into his open window. "Because you know what they say—" I pause and raise my brow suggestively.

"What do they say?"

"You can lead a horse to water. But you can't make 'em drink."

CHAPTER THIRTY-FOUR

Ruth

I'm sitting on the screened-in porch waiting for Roy to call. I
have to believe he'll pull through, even though it's possible I've
already obtained everything I need. Nevertheless, this is war, and
in war not only do you have to be smart, you have to come at
things from all angles. So I'm sitting and I'm praying and I'm
contemplating my next move when I look up and see the little girl
from next door in my garden again.

She's running through the yard, going from bed to bed,
picking petal after petal. When her hand is full, she drops them
into a tiny purse.

"Lily!" I call her name because her attacks on my garden are
beginning to feel personal. I hop off the rocker and take deep
strides in her direction. She doesn't stop picking.

"Lily," I say, touching her shoulder. "Stop."

"My daddy said it's okay," she tells me without turning around.

"Well, it's not okay. This is private property, and what you're doing is trespassing. And that is against the law."

She spins on her heel. "What does tres-pass-ing mean?"

"It means you're somewhere you don't belong."

She looks at me with a confused expression. "My daddy doesn't lie."

"Clearly, he does." I glance toward her house. "Where is your daddy, anyway?"

"He's not home right now."

"Where's your mother?"

"She's upstairs." She says this matter-of-factly, as though she doesn't have a care in the world.

"You need to go home. You shouldn't be outside by yourself."

"But I like it here." Her tone is sulky, but there's something more there. It's like she's already learned what she'll need to know to survive in this world as a woman. How to be manipulative. "And Daddy said he's buying this house. So I can play in the garden anytime I want."

FINALLY, I GET THE CHANCE TO SPEAK WITH ASHLEY ALONE. SURE, it's only because I corner her in the wine cellar. "How do you know the people next door?"

"What?"

"You heard me."

"I don't," she answers with her bottom lip jutted out. It's like looking at the little girl next door all grown up. "But I saw you making out with the cop."

"So?"

"So. He's not your type."

"You haven't been around long enough to know my type."

"What about Ryan?"

"What about him?"

"I'm working my ass off to get him here—to deliver him straight to you—and meanwhile you're trying to screw every guy in town."

"I suppose you might know a thing or two about that."

"I thought Davis told you." She smiles. "We're waiting until marriage."

I consider locking her down here. I wonder how long it would be before anyone checked. Then I notice the clipboard in her hand. "What are you doing?"

"I'm cataloging our selection of wines."

"They're not yours," I say. "Nothing around here is *yours*."

She flashes another smile. "Yet."

I glance at the clipboard. "Let me guess. Another one of your internet projects?"

"I just thought it would help. This way guests can order bottles straight to their rooms or buy some to take home. Plus, the party is tomorrow. And I just want to know where we stand."

"The wine down here is not for your engagement party."

"Right. That's why I'm cataloging it."

"I see." I glance over her shoulder at the list. "Well, I wanted to talk to you because I've been invested in a little internet project of my own."

She doesn't look at me when she speaks. "You're always so busy, Ruth."

"Does the name Chris ring a bell?"

Her eyes shift in the way that I can tell it does, and then she looks up. "Chris is a very common name."

"I guess."

"But maybe you've stolen from more than one. How would I know?"

"It's not what you think." She sighs heavily as she jots something down on her clipboard. When she's finished, she meets my gaze. "If you must know, I have a stalker."

"And here I thought you were a storyteller. I hope that's not the best you can do."

"You know how men can be," she says nonchalantly. "You slight them, in the tiniest way—you make them feel rejected—and they're capable of anything."

"He didn't sound crazy. But then looking at you, I guess anything is possible."

"Ruth—"

I take several steps forward and put my hand on the clipboard. "How much would it take for you to leave? What ten—twenty grand?"

She seems to try to gauge whether I'm serious, so I help her out. "I'm dead serious."

Her head cocks like she's offended. She isn't, and if she is, it's only by the dollar amount. "I love Davis. We're going to be married."

"Do you know how many men there are on the planet? You could have any one of them."

"You know," she says, with a tsk-ing sound. "Everyone says that. But when you narrow it down to age and desirable locations, it's actually a pretty small number. And that doesn't take looks—*or* the prosperity factor into consideration. Any smart woman knows the importance of being taken care of."

I wait for her to say more. But she only sighs wistfully. "So, thank you, Ruth. You've really given me a lot to think about."

"I bet I have."

Her bottom lip juts out. "Just one thing to think about—maybe that's why you're still single."

I imagine myself taking a wine bottle, cracking it over her skull and then using the broken bits to slit her pretty little throat.

"How about fifteen?"

"Fifteen grand?" Her nose scrunches up and her mouth twists before she relaxes her face. "Seems kind of lowball if you ask me."

I don't make a counteroffer. I wait her out.

Eventually, she shakes her head. "But tell you what. I'll think it over. First, I just have to know one thing…"

"What?"

"You didn't tell him where I am, did you?"

"Who—Chris?"

She shrugs. "If that's what he called himself."

"Sounds like you're two peas in a pod," I say, mimicking her smile. "And yeah, of course I did. He was just so interested."

Her face falls. "You made a huge mistake."

"Funny," I say. "Those are exactly the kind I tend to make."

I wait for her to respond and when she doesn't, it's my turn to shrug. "Whoopsie."

CHAPTER THIRTY-FIVE

Passerby

I've never been a big fan of parties, despite having grown up around them. This one I don't mind so much because it signifies things coming to an end, even though the point of it is supposed to celebrate a beginning.

Whatever the case, I'm just glad the con is almost over. I hate doing this to my family. I hate doing this to Ruth.

I didn't want to kill Bobby Holt, even though I kind of did. He deserved it. So did that bride's brother, even if he was a pain in the ass to kill.

But Julia has by far been the worst and the least premeditated of them all. It's why I couldn't do it. Not by myself. The others I did for Ashley. Because when you love someone the way I love her, you do whatever it takes to protect that person.

Those murders, I'd do those again, twice if I had to. But Julia was different. Visiting her in the hospital and holding that pillow over her face was the hardest thing I've ever had to do. I'm just glad Ashley was by my side, or I'm afraid I wouldn't have gone through with it. Hell, I couldn't even push her down the stairs hard enough to kill her. She changed my diapers. She even came to my Little League ball game once. I tried to explain this to Ashley, but she's the smart one. She knows all about loopholes and how if you leave them open, they're bound to be exploited.

And she was right. Julia was in the way. It's what she did. It's what she always did. She got too close.

Cole was the second worst, which is why I failed at killing him too. It was hard to pretend, to lie to Ashley, especially after chickening out on murdering my sister, not once but twice. What can I say? It's not as easy as they make it look on those true crime shows.

Killing your best friend is no joke. Even if, according to Ashley, the joke's on me, because I still have to take care of him, and now I've made it more likely that I'll get caught. She says if you want something done, you should do it right the first time. I'm not so sure that's how the saying goes, but she's pretty, so I let her believe.

This and I don't want to kill Cole, so I'm hoping that what they say about relationships is true. Compromise is key.

And still, all of that doesn't even touch the worst of it. There's my brother and what this is going to do to him. Ruth will be fine. She always is. I probably won't have to kill her. Ashley may just do it first.

I don't know if I blame her.

But Davis, that's a tough one. He's the only one to remain neutral in any of this. He's the only one of us that's truly innocent. Except that he was dumb enough to fall for the oldest trick in the book. He never would have agreed to sell Magnolia House without Ashley egging him on. I know what it means to fall in love with a woman like her, how it literally gives you the strength to do anything.

We met when I was out on a call. I changed out a flat for her, sent her on her way. But we kept in touch, and over the course of several months, we came up with the plan. See, the problem is, I'm kind of stuck here in this shit town. My job is here, and what I know is this: if you want to keep a woman like Ashley Parker, volunteer fire fighter pay isn't gonna do it. And once you land a woman like that, well, going back to anything less would be a shame. A real abomination. So I feel for Davis. You don't exactly get the cream of the crop around here. Which means I know that breaking the news to him that Ashley isn't really into him, and that this was all a scam, is going to kill him.

Metaphorically, if not literally.

The silver lining is that by that time we'll be long gone, Ashley and me.

We'll have money. We'll be able to go anywhere. After all, guilt can only travel so far. I highly doubt it shows up much on white, sandy beaches.

CHAPTER THIRTY-SIX

Ruth

This is not a job for an amateur. That much is obvious by the way my heart has lodged itself in my throat. I cover my mouth, partly because I'm in shock, partly because it will keep me from screaming. As tears prick my eyes, I bite down on my tongue in an attempt to keep them at bay. I am not a crier.

I push the door open further and enter the room. *Small hinges move heavy doors.* It's something my father used to say. I wish he were here now. He would know what to do.

My focus suddenly becomes very narrow, very clear. I stand frozen in place until I realize I ought to close the door behind me. I lock it for good measure, even though every fiber of my being is telling me to get out. *Turn around and run. Don't look back.*

Spoiler alert, that's not what I do.

I take another step forward.

The floor creaks underfoot as I move toward the desk, causing my heart to lurch further into my throat. After flipping on the lamp, I cross the room carefully. I reach for the curtains then realize I probably shouldn't. Guests have already begun trickling into the garden, and while I'm on the second floor, people have a way of seeing everything these days.

Not me, unfortunately. I should have checked this room earlier. Back when I sensed something was wrong. Back when I felt someone watching me. The times I heard funny noises.

I scan the room for answers, though it's pretty obvious what has happened. A double murder. That, or a murder-suicide. One way or the other, I have two bodies on my hands. Two bodies I have to get rid of and quick. Nothing spoils a party faster than a dead body. Two dead bodies and things go downhill twice as fast.

I hope you'll forgive my facetiousness. I'm awkward in situations that are outside of my control. But then again, I'm awkward most of the time.

The alarm clock on the nightstand catches my attention as it blinks on and off, flashing red, indicating that someone has unplugged it and plugged it back in. It reads 2:00 p.m.

I wish it was 2:00 p.m. I slide my phone from my back pocket and check the time. I have exactly twenty-seven minutes.

I can do this.

I have to do this.

There's a lot riding on me doing this.

I remind myself that I am not an amateur. I know how to get blood out of carpet, sheets, and fancy dresses. You name it, I'm sure I've tried it. I know how to scrub walls meticulously, but also carefully, so as not to rub the paint off. I know that when it comes to flooring, when a job is too big—like, say, this one—you don't bother trying to scrub, you simply cut swatches of carpet out. It never looks quite right, even if you manage to find a suitable match, but a piece of furniture, carefully placed, or a rug, will take care of that.

Here, I don't know. There's an awful lot of blood. The plush carpet that was just installed last January? Toast. I'm guessing drywall will have to be removed. One thing is for sure, someone in this room fought like hell. I wonder which of them it was. Was it both?

I clench my fists and then stretch my fingers. The mattress is a goner, for sure. I can't afford this. Although, there isn't time to think about that now. This requires a quick fix, a Band-Aid, *anything* that will buy me some time. Not enough time to call professionals, although that's certainly what I'd prefer.

Like The Rolling Stones said: You can't always get what you want.

And anyway, I can't afford professionals, either.

I know what you're thinking. You're thinking, I could do what most people in my shoes would do. I could call the police.

Trust me, that's probably the least affordable option.

There are lives at stake, and livelihoods, which are sometimes one and the same, more so than you'd think.

So here I am, standing over two dead bodies, surveying the blood splatter, wondering if I'll ever be able to find wallpaper this pretty again. It's like two paths diverged in a wood. I know this isn't a Robert Frost poem, but bear with me, it's my favorite, and at this moment, my mind is going to strange places. It's the shock, a protective mechanism. You wouldn't believe the things our brains and our bodies can do. They can perform miraculous feats in the name of preservation.

If only it had worked for these two.

Anyway, two paths diverged in a wood...and here I am, staring down both of them. Only, I know what's in store; I know where they lead. Path number one is the right choice, of course. The obvious choice. The good choice. The moral high ground. Path number two is the choice only a desperate person would make. A fool's trip. One that leads to nowhere good. And yet...*what choice do I have?*

I could try to explain myself. But you wouldn't understand. No one can possibly understand. Not until they've walked a mile in my shoes, and believe me, they wouldn't want that, either. My shoes are currently taking on blood faster than the *Titanic* took on water.

Deep breath in. Deep breath out.

I can do this.

I have to do this.

I wring my hands out, wiping my sweaty palms on my shorts. Sweat slides down my spine. *No, not a job for an amateur at all.*

Thankfully, I've read up on the bio-recovery industry. Most people refer to it as crime scene cleanup—biohazard remediation—trauma scene restoration. Point is—they're the people who come out and clean blood, bodily fluids, and other potentially dangerous materials following less than desirable situations. It's a specialty. A career path people actually chose. So many possibilities, when you think of it. So many paths one can take. I can almost hear my father saying, *your imagination is your only limitation.*

He may have been wrong about that, judging by the state of this room. The business of death cleanup requires a cold disposition and a strong stomach. And unfortunately, I have only one of the two.

What I also don't have is time.

Twenty-four minutes. The clock is running down, and I have no timeouts left. Time marches on, reminding me even the best-laid plans rarely go off without a hitch.

Hitches. Now there's something I'm familiar with. I just hadn't expected one of this magnitude. *That* was my mistake. But it wasn't the first one, and looking around, it isn't going to be the last.

I slide my phone into my back pocket again and open the closet. I could stuff them in there. Maybe. Unfortunately, old houses have small closets, and it would take quite a bit of effort to make them fit. And perhaps a few broken bones.

For a second, I think I might actually be losing it and I wonder if this is what they mean by the term *psychotic break.* I consider calling someone. *But who?* What kind of friend do you call to get you out of a jam like this?

Problem is, I know exactly what kind of friend.

But I won't go there. *I can't go there.*

Bad things happen when I go there.

Things worse than this.

You wouldn't think anything could be worse than this.

But again, you wouldn't understand.

I hope you're not offended. I'm not saying you're stupid or anything.

It's not you.

Most people wouldn't understand.

Probably not even these two, I tell myself, and then I don't know why I do it, but I lean down, pull back the covers, and really take them in. The waxy skin, the bloated faces, or what's left of them anyway, the transfixed eyes. You might think they look peaceful, but you would be wrong. This is the stuff nightmares are made of. And I see many in my future.

My phone dings. The sound startles me, and I practically leap into the bed with them. My knee bumps the mattress, and a hand flops over the side, brushing my bare skin. Every expletive I know floods my mind as I dance back. They'd come pouring out of my mouth, but I'm too afraid to open it. My phone dings again. I stare at the hand and think: *this can't be real.* Then I back away and read the text. *Where are you? I can't believe this is happening. Finally.*

He has no idea.

This is sick, he writes.

I look around the room. *Truly.*

Sick as in a BFD.

I know what you mean; I text back. He likes it when I'm up on my acronyms. He is not one who likes to explain himself, and he reads minds like it's his profession.

It is a big effing deal.

It's not every day that you hold an engagement party of this magnitude at your venue, but that is exactly what is happening in precisely twenty-one minutes. The entire town will be here. What a disaster this is going to turn out to be. Looking back, I should have said no. I tried to say no. I did say no.

It didn't work. And anyway, as for him being here, it was a favor to make up for that other favor.

My phone chimes again. *Thank God for small favors!*

I shake my head. It appears a favor is what got me into this, and a favor is going to have to be what gets me out.

CHAPTER THIRTY-SEVEN

Ruth

M y hands shake. Cold sweats sweep over me. Perspiration dampens the small of my back, the edges of my hairline, *everything*. I have to get out of this room.

The walls feel like they're closing in on me. It's hot as hell in here, and it feels like I'm in one of those fun houses at the festival where the floor shifts and the walls are made of mirrors and nothing is as it seems.

This must be what shock feels like. In every sense of the word. The fear animals must experience right before they're slaughtered. I will probably live. Not only because I still have the ability to run, but because this isn't about me. I've just gotten caught up in the middle.

I don't know how this is going to turn out, only that I am most likely about to have to sell my soul to the devil. Any minute now, Roy is going to take those stairs light-footed and two at a time.

He's going to find me in here. Me and two dead bodies. And when he does, I have to be prepared. I'm going to have to cut a deal.

I will have to marry him and have his babies.

Assuming he'll have me.

Whatever it takes.

I consider my options. I consider all the ways I could get rid of him. I could put in a 9-1-1 call about kids fighting down at the beach. I could mention teenagers vandalizing the courthouse. Or suggest a welfare check way out on the outskirts of town. I could do a number of things—or I could simply face the music and let the chips fall where they may.

As I contemplate this, my eyes shift toward the bed. I can't help noticing that Ashley looks good naked, even dead. I know it's a weird thing to think at a time like this, but this is how women are. Everything is a comparison. Standards of beauty are drilled into us at an early age, and that conditioning is hard to escape. Or maybe it's just the things that seem forbidden tend to look the best.

I take it my brother knew a thing or two about that.

The problem is, looking at Ashley forces me to look at him, and I can't bear it. Not again. I saw his face, or what was left of it, and once was enough. I half expect him to leap up, to tell me this is all a joke, a delicious prank that we'll recant over Thanksgiving dinner for years to come. Everyone will laugh. Sometimes even me.

Please, I plead with God. With the universe. *Don't let this be real.*

Johnny has always been the strong one. The older, protective brother. The one with all the answers. And now, he isn't saying anything, when there's a whole lot I need him to say.

For one, *how did this happen?*

Not in a trillion years did I ever see this coming.

But also, *how* did I not see it?

The question reminds me of a conversation I had with Cole once after we'd made love in this very bed. It was just a few days after Ashley arrived, a day or two after the Watermelon Festival. Casually, I'd asked if he had any ideas on how I might go about getting rid of her.

"I don't know," he told me. Knowing him, he probably referenced *The Art of War* or some other book, but if so, I can't recall. I only remember what he said exactly as it applied to my situation. He stroked my hair and said, "Stick your head up and get it cut off, and you serve as a cautionary example. People will be terrified of the result and will cower in fear. You have to keep cool and resist intelligently."

"What does that even mean?" I asked.

"It means that every bit of resistance in the system drags it and slows it down. Eventually, with enough resistance, it overheats and grinds to a stop. *That* is the time for action. *That* is the time to make your move."

I looked at him like he'd lost his mind, like he might as well have been speaking Romanian. "What are you talking about?"

He studied me closely before he answered in that keen way of his. It probably seemed to him like I wasn't all that interested, but I couldn't have been more riveted. With a charming, easy smile, he whispered, "Subvert. Evade. Survive."

"Sounds like you've been reading too much dystopia."

"Civilization is not a very good paint job," he said with a shake of his head. "Three days without food and it will flake off. We are predators, Ruth, and we will hunt. Prey is anyone, or anything, who can't defend themselves. Dystopian literature barely touches exactly how bad it can get."

It may seem like what I'm saying, like our conversation, has nothing to do with finding my brother and Ashley Parker bludgeoned to death.

But, I assure you, it has every bit to do with it.

Unfortunately, unpacking *that* isn't my most pressing issue right now.

Now, I have to figure out how I'm going to keep people out of this room. Outside of hanging crime scene tape, I'm not exactly sure how I'm going to accomplish that seeing as more than half the town is about to descend down on this house, and there's nothing like a locked door to make nosey people want to open it and peek inside.

You wouldn't think any of them would want to see this.

You'd be surprised.

Although, before any of that happens, I have to find Davis.

My guess? He's wandering around here somewhere, all zombie-like, his clothes covered in blood. God, I hope he's smarter than that.

The thought conjures a memory of us as kids. We'd rush home from school and sneak up to this room to watch recaps of the OJ Simpson trial on the old big box television that used to sit in the corner.

I doubt Mama and Daddy had any idea that's what we were doing, because if they had, they never would have allowed it.

It makes me wonder if Davis learned anything.

Me, I learned this is a room of many uses.

It could hold the secrets of secrets.

Although, I suppose you always get caught, one way or another. Karma has a way of evening the score, which means I'd better find Davis before Roy or anyone else does. I've lost one brother. I'm terrified of what's going to become of the other.

CHAPTER THIRTY-EIGHT

Ruth

One thing I've figured out, you can't have better standards for a person than they have for their own self. That is proven when I walk into the kitchen and find Davis sitting at the table with his head in his hands. The kitchen is an absolute disaster. I'd been readying things for the party when I realized that I'd forgotten to pick up my dress at the seamstress. I rushed out the door, drove like a bat out of hell, just to reach her shop as she was locking up.

She didn't look thrilled to see me, but she handed over the dress, and she was kind enough to allow me to try it on, even making a slight alteration while I waited. I take note of Davis and begin to clear clutter from one of the counters. It's pointless, all things considered, but it helps with the nervous energy and it gives me something to do with my hands.

Meanwhile, Davis doesn't look up at me, or acknowledge my presence. He sits with a bottle of red in front of him, unopened, and he mumbles. I'm not sure what he's saying, but it sounds a lot like the Lord's Prayer.

His hands tremble. His fingernails are caked in blood. "I didn't mean to do it, really, I didn't."

"You need to get showered and changed," I tell him, sliding into full-on big sister mode. "Guests are starting to arrive. And we can't have them seeing you like this."

I don't mean any of this literally. Obviously, that would be tampering with evidence. I only mean that we need to get him somewhere a little more private, at least until I can figure out what to do, or if that's what I *want* to do.

"Where's Roy?" I ask. It's a rhetorical question designed to shake Davis out of his stupor. I glance toward the window, feeling more than a little relieved not to find him in this kitchen.

If Roy isn't in here, and he isn't upstairs, the next most likely place for me to find him is in the parlor, standing over the pool table, weighing his next move. But then, I realize there's some part of me that suspects that might not be the case and that Davis's lack of response indicates something far worse than I'd imagined.

"I didn't mean it."

"It's okay," I say softly. "I don't blame you."

"You should."

"Davis, listen to me. I need to know if you've seen Roy. He texted that he was downstairs."

I glance down at the knife on the table in front of him.

He rubs at his eyes with the palms of his hands. Still, he refuses to look at me. "I think you should leave, Ruth."

"I can't leave. We're having a party. Like right now."

"I don't want to hurt anyone else."

"You wouldn't, Davis. Of course, you wouldn't."

He looks up at me with sharp, intelligent eyes that crease slightly at the corners from years of easy going smiles. He doesn't look like himself. He doesn't look like a zombie, either. Quite frankly, he looks like someone capable of murder. "You saw them?"

"Yes," I say. "I saw them."

"Johnny never liked her."

"I don't know. I guess he liked her well enough."

"You!" he shouts. He sits upright in his chair and toys with the knife. "You never liked her."

"Davis," I say, backing away. "I'm going to ask you one more time. Where is Roy?"

He scoffs, and I realize how much I sound like my mother. His eyes narrow, and when he speaks, he does it in a way that scares me. "What's it to you?"

"I don't want anything to happen to you. If anyone is going to handle this situation, it needs to be Roy."

"I'm a dead man, Ruth. You should go now."

"It's understandable," I tell him. "What you've done. Anyone would have that reaction—after what you found."

He eyes me with a furrowed brow. "I didn't protect her. Not from Johnny and not from him."

"Davis—"

"This is my fault." He breaks down in hurried sobs. "It is. All of it, it's my fault."

An uproar of laughter comes from the foyer. Guests chat on the other side of the kitchen door. The noise level tells me they're increasing in number, and it's just a matter of time before one of them comes looking for me.

"What am I going to do, Ruth?" He cries. "Just tell me what to do?"

Just beyond the top of Davis's head, I see people congregating in the garden. I want to tell him that I tried that already. That I saw this ending badly a thousand ways to sundown. But I know that won't help. I know it's too late to matter. So, I say, "We can fix this," even though I don't think we can.

My lie calms him, albeit only momentarily. "Maybe we should call Mike," he tells me. "He knows the law. He'll know what to do."

He's right about this. You should never make a statement to police before you've had the chance to talk to your attorney. Police have a job to do and you need to be cooperative, but you don't want to say too much because anything you say will be used against you. "If you'll tell me where Roy is, I'll have him get rid of the guests. Then, the rest, we can figure out."

"They'll eat me alive in prison. You have to know that."

He's right about this, too. I know it without a doubt. I also know that my little brother has proven twice recently that he isn't that good in a fight. It makes me sad for him. If only he'd heeded my warning back when he still had a chance.

"It'll all work out," I lie. "I don't know how, but it will."

"This isn't *Runaway Bride*, Ruth. Ashley's dead." He slips as he says her name and the sobbing returns.

"I know," I answer, speaking under my breath. "I saw."

"I should have protected her."

I don't know what he means, and I don't think to ask because that's when I hear a commotion coming from the cellar.

My brother's eyes grow wider than I've ever seen them. "Oh, God. He's up."

"Who? Roy?" My eyes search his.

This time it's my eyes that widen. "You locked him in the cellar?"

"I didn't know what else to do."

CHAPTER THIRTY-NINE

Ruth

The kitchen doors swing open and Cole comes barreling through. He appears to be every bit as surprised to see me as I am to see him, which makes little sense given that he's in my house.

"What are you doing here?" I ask at the same time he says, "Johnny invited me."

"You could've said no." I know this is the absolute worst time for an argument. I have much bigger fish to fry, but just seeing his face, I can't help myself.

"Where is he?"

When I don't offer an immediate response, Cole turns toward the door. "Forget it. I'll find him."

"He's out," I say. "On a call."

"Great." He gives me the once over. "In that case, I'll wait outside."

Cole pushes the kitchen door open, giving me one last glance over his shoulder. Suddenly, he pivots on his heel. As he looks from me to Davis, his entire demeanor changes.

I watch his expression shift as recognition takes hold. He stares at the butcher knife in Davis's hand, and he realizes he didn't just walk in on an argument between two siblings.

With a nod, I say, "You should wait outside."

Cole surprises me by sliding a chair out from under the table and taking a seat. I stand frozen in place, my feet half ready to run, half bolted to the floor as he places his hands on the table and spreads his fingers wide. I know Cole carries a pistol, so the move is generous on his part, and also, in my opinion, stupid.

I won't lie. This sort of stunt makes me fall in love with him a little bit. I hate us both for it.

Cole doesn't think he's in danger. But he didn't see what I saw upstairs. Davis doesn't just kill people, he resets their faces.

Another booming sound comes from the cellar.

His chin juts toward Davis. "Johnny down there?"

I shake my head.

My brother tightens his grip on the knife.

I wonder how quick on the draw Cole is.

I wonder whether I want him to be quick enough.

CHAPTER FORTY

Ruth

A single light bulb dangles from the ceiling. It sways from side to side like a pendulum, and as it moves, it flickers on and off. It comes to life before dying out again.

Cole did not draw his weapon. He didn't have to. Davis volunteered to show us what's in the cellar. It could be a trap, which is why I move down the old creaky stairs slowly and cautiously, deeply afraid of what I am going to find. Deeply afraid of never seeing the light of day again.

I don't think that my brother would hurt me. But fear makes people do stupid things, things they wouldn't ordinarily do.

My heart picks up pace, something I didn't think was possible.

Davis is two steps behind me. And just behind him, Cole urges us both on.

When we reach the bottom step, Davis cuts in front of me. He walks over to the wall of bottles. I watch as his fingertips, caked in dried blood, slide over the labels. He stops when he finds one that is familiar. A simple smile passes across his features as he slides it out.

He turns to leave, as though this is the reason we've come, as though everything that's happened hasn't. "Where is Roy?" I demand, and Davis stops as though he remembers. He glances around the shadowy cellar. It's an unsettling part of the house, always has been.

Davis stands very still and watches the edge of the cellar where the light doesn't quite touch. Just beyond that is the door that leads to the small room where Mama used to store canned goods, and Daddy liked to keep money.

As my eyes adjust to the dim light, I see that just in front of the door lays a lump in the exact shape of a human. The light swings this way and that way, until Cole catches it in his hand. He fiddles with it until it's steady and the room is illuminated.

"Roy?" I say, taking strides in that direction. I kneel next to the figure on the floor. In his right hand is a baton, and he rears it back. Just when I am certain he is going to strike me, Davis moves forward and kicks it out of his hand.

Cole steps forward and takes my brother by the arm. He forces him to the ground. "Stay," he says, and Davis complies.

I check Roy over, or at least as much as one can in the dark. "Are you okay?"

He's kind of going in and out of consciousness, which is maybe why he doesn't answer. *God, let him be okay.* Killing a cop is no joke, and Roy is my friend. It's my fault he's here. Blood drips from his temple, and one hand is cuffed to a pipe. His gun is missing from his holster. This would be really difficult to make look like an accident. "Roy," I say, slapping his cheek. "Roy, talk to me."

"He's fine," Davis coughs. "He just took a little tumble down the stairs."

My eyes land on my brother. "What the fuck?"

"I know," Davis says. "It was stupid. But he saw me covered in blood, and I didn't know what to do."

I look over at Cole, who is searching for something. Hopefully, it's the gun. Above us, there are footsteps. Party-goers have made their way into the kitchen.

"Davis," I say, saving Cole the trouble of searching for a needle in a haystack. "Where is the gun?"

He points upward.

"In the kitchen?" It can't be. "I would have seen it."

"Yeah, well," Davis tells me with a scoff. "I guess there are a lot of things we don't see. Not unless we know to look for them."

Roy stirs. I place my hand on his shoulder. He reaches up to touch the gash in his forehead with his free hand. "Your brother is in deep shit," he mumbles as he cups his head.

A chill sweeps over me. "I know."

I turn to Davis. "Where's the key to the cuffs?"

He shrugs. "How should I know?"

"The key is in my wallet," Roy says, shifting. He winces as he moves. "I'm going to need you to hand me my radio."

As I move to empty his pocket, my foot connects with something on the floor just beyond where he is crouched. My eyes shift, and it takes me by surprise when Roy reaches up and takes my chin in his hand. "I wouldn't look if I were you."

I should listen, but I don't. "Cole, shift the light this way, would you?"

He does and then I wish he hadn't. What I see is gruesome, but from the chin upward, it's also just a young man with a forgettable face. Roy releases the grip he has on my chin. I take a deep breath in and let it out. "Who is he?"

"That's Chris Larsen," Davis says flatly.

My stomach sinks like I'm on the downward slope of a very fast roller coaster.

"Who's Chris Larsen?" Cole asks.

"Ashley's ex," Davis and Roy say at the same time. I don't

answer because there's a lump in my throat that's too big to speak around.

"You asked me to do some checking," Roy tells me with a groan. "And I did…"

It seems a little late for this information, but as I search his wallet for the key to free him, I let him talk. "She had a restraining order against him."

"He tried to kill her," Davis says.

My fingers make contact with the key. I fish it out and hold it between my fingers. "What's he doing down here?"

Davis's eyes meet mine. "He finally succeeded."

Cole bends over the man. With one hand he holds a flashlight, with the other he covers his nose and mouth. "He's dead."

Davis chokes out a sob. "He killed them. He literally beat them to death."

I don't believe him. Not for a minute. I want to know how he ended up down here. It doesn't add up, and I want more detail. But this doesn't feel like the time to ask.

"He's damn well nearly decapitated," Roy says.

Davis nods. "I wanted to see the look in his eyes when he knew it was over."

CHAPTER FORTY-ONE

Ruth

It's difficult to explain what it was like coming out of that cellar. For the most part, what took place after was, and still is, a blur. It could be the spectacle aspect of it that has caused me to block it out. No one likes to sit with shame, and to say the entire town was watching would be putting it mildly. And if recent events are any indication, they won't be looking elsewhere anytime soon.

As they say in the press, "If it bleeds, it leads." Killing someone, no matter if you claim it was in self-defense, makes a great news piece. Kill several people, mix in a little love triangle, an allegedly deranged ex and well, you have all the ingredients for a real show. Gossip and speculation are one thing Jester Falls excels at.

That doesn't mean I've been able to put it out of my mind entirely, just because my memory is hazy. Of course, I haven't. It's in my face every single hour of every single day.

That night brings up a lot of things. I wake sometimes, sitting straight up in bed, in the dead of night, certain I see flashing lights. I dream about standing around, watching Magnolia House being roped off with yellow tape. It's always the same. Someone wraps a scratchy blanket around my shoulders as flashes catch my eye from the second floor. The nightmare is the same as the reality. It takes me a second to understand what I am seeing when I look up at that window. Flashes from the camera photographing my brother's corpse. It's the strangest things you remember. It's the strangest things that haunt your dreams.

The usual characters make their appearance. Ryan Jenkins and his lovely wife. The thoughts about those people, they don't change. I remember thinking that Ashley had, in fact, pulled off what she'd set out to do and how ironic that was.

That night outside Magnolia House, police pushed us back, beyond the yellow tape. Ryan and his wife stood close to where Cole and I were. At this point, Davis had already been placed in cuffs, and Roy was being assessed in the back of an ambulance. I turned to look over my shoulder, and my eyes caught his for the briefest of moments. His wife was leaning into him, whispering in his ear. I couldn't hear most of what was being said, just this one thing. She said, "I bet you're glad you didn't marry into this family."

That was when our eyes locked, Ryan's and mine. He held my gaze for a beat, and then he looked back at her. "Huh?"

"I said, this family, they're crazy."

"Oh," he told her. "Yeah."

Cole squeezed my arm. "It's going to be okay. Not tonight. But it will be."

Tears snuck out of the corners of my eyes. "How do you know?"

"I don't."

"This is a fucking nightmare."

"Yes," he said. "For me, too."

CHAPTER FORTY-TWO

Ruth

For a second, I think I might be actually losing it, and I wonder if this is what they mean by the term *psychotic break*. I consider calling someone. *But who?* What kind of friend do you call to get you out of a jam like this?

Problem is, I know exactly what kind of friend.

But I won't go there. *I can't go there.*

Bad things happen when I go there.

Things worse than being questioned in a small, stuffy, dimly lit room with a lead investigator that looks like she's barely a day out of college.

She apologizes for my loss and then she says, "It can't get any worse for you, Ms. Channing, can it?"

You wouldn't think anything could be worse than this. "I don't know," I tell her. But I do know. Prison would be worse.

She blinks several times. I don't know if this is a tactic, only that it works. Her rapid blinking, it makes me want to talk. "I can imagine how you must be feeling."

I offer a nod. It's the best I can manage. She flip-flops so much it makes me dizzy. One second she's warm and compassionate, the next it's like she's taunting me. It's like she's poking at a bear in a cage. "Hm."

"This has to be really hard for you."

"Yeah." *But again, like I said, you wouldn't understand.*

I expect her to continue, to say something, to say anything, but she doesn't. Not for several minutes. She just sits there stoically, blinking and not saying anything, and I don't understand. What is she doing? Is she trying to wait me out?

"Is there someone I can call?"

"No."

I watch as she crosses and uncrosses her legs. She does some more blinking, and I wonder what her family is like. I wonder what led her to a job like this. "Is there anything I can do to help you feel more comfortable?"

"No." *It's not you.* I tell her there isn't anything she can do, though I've said it all before. I've told the story. One way and then another, and still, she isn't satisfied.

"You think I don't understand?"

I shrug. *I hope you're not offended. I'm not saying you're stupid or anything.*

"Wait." She holds up one hand. "I know," she says, right before she repeats what I've told her, word for word. "Most people wouldn't understand."

I shrug again. *Bingo.*

The less I speak, the better.

She empties her foam cup, slurping every drop. When she places the cup on the table, she jiggles it as though coffee might manifest from out of thin air. Not that I blame her. She's making a point.

I'm wasting her time. I figure she's getting paid either way, and at the moment, I don't exactly have gainful employment to go back to. All I've got is time.

"You're not under arrest, Ruth. You don't have to answer my questions."

This, I know. I'm also not falling for this good cop, bad cop shtick, either. I remember what Cole said to me, standing outside my house as they strung the crime scene tape. He looked at me and he placed his hands on my shoulders. Then he leaned in like his life depended on it and he said, *"You'll think you're too smart to fall for their routine, but you're not. You'll be upset and you'll want to talk, especially to anyone who appears sympathetic. Law enforcement officers are not necessarily your enemy, but they're not your friend either. Shut up. Talk to your lawyer—clear it with Mike—before you make any statement of any kind."*

"Okay," I told him.

He searched my face. "Promise me."

"I'm terrible at promises. You know that."

I look at the young woman seated in front of me and I say, "I'm terrible at promises."

"How so?"

"I promised Mama and Daddy that I'd take care of them. And now one is under arrest and the other is dead."

She looks at me like she understands, but she doesn't.

"Do you have any brothers?"

She nods. "Yes, one."

I say nothing in response. I let the sentiment hang in the air. She may not understand, but I've just leveled the playing field some.

"Did you know Ms. Jepson had a restraining order against Chris Larsen when you reached out to him?"

"I told you I didn't."

"Were you aware that Ms. Jepson was sleeping with your brother?" She clears her throat, realizing that clarification is necessary. Her discomfort brings me a sense of enjoyment I haven't felt in a long time. "With Johnny?"

"No."

"Did you suspect?"

I think about all the times I felt like someone was watching me. All the times I heard noises coming from upstairs and how when I called no one answered. I shake my head. "No."

"Did Davis know?"

"I don't think so."

"You've stated that Ms. Jepson wanted to sell Magnolia House. That she went so far as to find a buyer."

I don't see what this has to do with her murder, but I'm afraid she might. She's trying to connect dots that aren't there. "That's correct."

"He was your neighbor. This potential buyer?"

"He was a developer. Looking for a property grab."

"To your knowledge, did Ms. Jepson have a relationship with him?"

"I have no idea. She only told me they spoke once."

"Did Davis think they were having a relationship?"

"If he did, he never told me."

"The family moved after the murders?"

"It lowered the property value, I assume."

"As you mentioned before, it's your opinion that Ms. Jepson was using your brother to urge him to sell your bed and breakfast?"

"Johnny wanted the money."

"He told you this?"

"More than once."

"What do you think, Ruth?" Her eyes narrow. "I want your opinion. What do you think Ms. Jepson stood to gain from any of this?"

Opinions aren't facts. She knows this. I think about her question for a long moment before answering. "I don't know. Money.

A comfortable life. Love. Or what she thought was love." *What everyone wants.* I pause just long enough to shrug, and that's when the hypothetical answers end and the real one begins. "I don't know. Only she can answer that."

"Except she's dead."

She says this to try to goad a reaction out of me. It almost works. I know Ashley is dead. I saw. Believe me, I saw. "All I know is that she was obviously running from something. And that something found her."

"Ah, that's right." She toys with a bracelet on her left wrist, and I can see that she's running out of patience. This is good and bad. It means she's losing steam, but also that she's about to play hardball. "Davis suggests he walked in on Ms. Jepson on Johnny *after* Mr. Larson murdered the two of them. But the evidence doesn't show this to be the case."

"So I'm told." I glance at the clock and back at her. I think about Magnolia House and what I would be doing right now if I wasn't here. "I don't know. I wasn't there."

"Do you think Davis killed your brother and Ms. Jepson?"

Her question does not surprise me. The particular wording she uses does not surprise me. She wants me to be emotional. When emotions run high, intellect runs low.

But I will not give her what she wants, at least not fully. It does not surprise me I'm being treated like a criminal. I assumed that I'd be handcuffed, placed prone on the ground, locked in the back of a cruiser, possibly even jailed. It takes time to sort out the truth of any crime, and I was aware it would be likely that the police would do any or all of these things. So I don't take it personally. I don't resist or argue. Even though I want to. Even though those responses would be natural, even instinctual, I know that the best way to make this go away is to cooperate until things are sorted out in my favor. Which they will be. So I am direct, but respectful. "Like I said, I wasn't there."

"You were picking up your dress."

"Yes. I had it altered for the party."

"Did he tell you what happened in the cellar?"

"Roy?" I know who she is talking about, but I can also play her game.

"Davis." She leans in and rests her elbows on the rickety table. "Did he tell you how he killed Chris Larsen?"

"No." I don't tell her I could see it for myself—that his head was barely attached to his body or that the floor was coated, and is *still* somewhat coated in that man's blood.

"Did he say anything?"

"Who?" *Facts are important.*

"Davis."

"He said he was dead."

"Anything else?"

I glance at the clock on the wall once more and back at her. It's obvious what she's trying to do, and I won't allow her to try my case on the spot. I know from years of hanging around Roy that police have more than one way to get you to talk. Aside from good cop/bad cop, she's challenging the use of lethal force. I want to argue my case—or Davis's case, she's still deciding—but I won't. I'll keep my mouth shut. I'm not a lawyer and I'm not in a court-room. Not yet, anyway.

"Ms. Channing. Did Davis say anything when he took you into the cellar?"

I wanted to see the look in his eyes when he knew it was over. I give it several seconds before I shake my head. "Not that I recall."

EPILOGUE

Ruth

Eight years later

D addy used to say a house divided against itself cannot
stand. He'd look at other families, usually guests, and
proclaim: That family is going to eat themselves alive from the
inside out.

I didn't know what he meant back then, but I do now.

I found Johnny's notebooks in the workshop, detailing what he
did. How he tried to kill me. It took several days for detectives to
complete their investigation and clear the house, but once they
did, it was slightly less messy.

I did not share the contents of those notebooks with the
police. Sometimes less is more.

A house divided against itself cannot stand.

I'm just glad Daddy isn't around to see what's become of us. It's not all bad, but it's also not what it could have been. Cole calls my name, and I push myself forward, up out of the rocker, leading with my burgeoning belly.

"Look," Shelby says. "Look at me!" She's grinning from ear to ear, and she speaks animatedly as I waddle over to her. She has her Daddy's smile and her uncle's translucent eyes. It makes me ache for Johnny in a way I hadn't known possible. It's a tricky thing, and it's nearly impossible to describe how you can hold such love and such hate for a person, and sometimes in equal proportion.

"I can do it!" she exclaims, jumping up and down.

Several members of the staff have lined up on the porch to watch. "Look at you!" Ms. Eve squeals. She's not Julia, but we love her. And Shelby doesn't know any different anyhow.

"We have a bike rider in the house," Cole announces proudly. If you asked him, he'd tell you we named our daughter after his favorite car. Me, I'd tell you the truth. She's named after my favorite character in *Steel Magnolias.* How we ended up together is anyone's guess and also what seemed like a forgone conclusion. I hadn't meant to get pregnant, but I hadn't *not* meant to either.

When I told him, the first words out of his mouth were as I expected. *Marry me.*

I hadn't wanted to hear any of it. "I feel like this is the same conversation we keep having over and over."

"Great." He ignored me completely. "So? What do you say? You wanna come live out in the woods with me?"

"What, like happily ever after?"

"Probably not like that. But I think we'd do okay."

"Magnolia House is my home, Cole. Always has been. Always will be."

"Yeah," he said. "But now it's two against one." He laid his hand on my stomach and looked up at me with that charming smile of his. "The way it's looking, the odds are stacked against you."

"I never perform better under any other condition."

He laughed. "Now, that I believe."

As the sun sets, our daughter looks up at me and tugs at my hand, anchoring me in the present. "Daddy says we can take the training wheels off tomorrow."

"You're still getting the hang of it, honey. I think we'd better give it a minute."

"But," she pouts. "I want to show Uncle Davey."

"Davis," I say, patting her head. "Uncle Davis."

"He's coming." She looks at me suspiciously, as though perhaps I've forgotten. "Tomorrow? Remember, you said."

"That's right."

"Is it tomorrow yet?" She has asked this nearly every hour on the hour for the past several days. At seven, her concept of time is still a little shaky.

"Almost."

SOMETIMES, USUALLY AT NIGHT, SHELBY ASKS ME TO TELL HER about Uncle Johnny. I usually defer to Cole, but I think about Johnny a lot. It's hard not to. Business is booming again. We rebranded, though not intentionally. It has been said and written that two lovers haunt the room they were murdered in. The story draws a lot of attention. Most of it unwanted.

That room is locked off. We do not rent that room, not ever.

But it doesn't stop people from asking or from trying.

As for it being haunted, that's an interesting subject. *I* am haunted. So who's to say? And I will admit that strange things do sometimes occur. Sometimes in the dead of night, I wake to the sound of a woman laughing. And while time has faded the memory at its edges, I do know that laugh and the first time I heard it, sitting at my kitchen table on a warm summer's day.

Davis was indicted on murder charges. They sentenced him to seventeen years, but with good behavior, he's out after seven.

I'm both hopeful and dreading seeing him. Our relationship is a bit strained on account that I wouldn't mortgage Magnolia House to the hilt to pay for his defense. Davis made his bed, and he had to lie in it.

And I knew that not only would I not allow anything to take this house from me, but that when the dust settled, Davis would need a place to call home.

So when he called two days ago from the road and asked if I minded if he headed this way upon his release, I couldn't say anything other than yes.

He arrives just after lunch. I watch him from the kitchen window as he steps out of the car. He looks older than the last time I saw him, but has more pep in his step. Being a free man has that effect, I'm sure.

I visited him in prison as much as I could, but then Shelby came along, and now there will be another baby soon. I have a business to run, and seeing him in an orange jumpsuit was harder than I thought. Eventually, I came up with enough excuses, and eventually he stopped asking.

I make my way from the kitchen to the front door on shaky footing. I don't know what to expect. Through the screen door, I see a hint of golden hair and my breath catches.

As I step out onto the porch, I open my mouth to call for Shelby and Cole, but nothing comes out.

"Ruth," Davis nods. He pulls a woman from behind his back, like a magician pulling a rabbit out of a hat. "This is Cassie."

She reaches out and extends her hand in my direction. "Cassandra."

Cassandra is a lot of things. Young and beautiful and a dead ringer for Ashley Parker.

I have so many questions. I don't ask them though; I let my eyes do the talking, and I figure all things come in time.

Over tea and a weak imitation of Julia's pimento cheese dip, Cassandra relays the story of how she and Davis met.

It takes me a few minutes to set everything right in my mind. I could blame pregnancy brain, but I don't think it's that. "So what, you were like pen-pals?"

Davis stirs his tea and then takes a sip. "Well, it was a little different than that."

My head cocks. "Different how?"

"We had internet. We emailed."

Cassandra looks at my brother and then at me. "Sometimes we wrote."

"We're getting married," Davis says, popping a cracker in his mouth. "And we were hoping to do it here."

"At Magnolia House?"

A wide grin spreads across my brother's face. "I can't imagine anywhere else."

"So you'll be staying for a while, then?"

He nods. "In the guest house, if that's okay."

I watch as Davis stands and walks over to the sink. He stares out the window, and I wonder how much prison has changed him, if any. "There they are," he says abruptly, catching me off guard. I follow his gaze: Cole and Shelby coming up the road hand in hand.

"They must have gone down to the beach while I was napping."

Davis doesn't answer. He bolts out the door and jogs down the drive toward them.

"Davey tells me you're having a boy."

My eyes turn away from the window. "Yes."

"You must be so excited!"

"We are."

"Davey?" I ask, with the tilt of my chin.

"Hmm?"

"You called him Davey. Did he tell you to call him that?"

"That's his nickname, right?"

213

My brows rise, and I press my lips together. I let that be my answer.

"I mean, that's what everyone calls him?"

"Not me."

She leans forward, resting her chin in her hand. "Huh."

I clear our plates from the table. "How long have you known my brother?" I am inclined to hold up air quotes as I utter the word known, but I'm very pregnant, and I'm very tired.

This, and I don't yet know what she knows.

I wonder if Davis told her about his brother and how he murdered people. I wonder if he told her that people will probably never know the truth, not for certain, even if they suspect, because I never told anyone about the notebooks I found in the workshop. No one except Davis.

Not even my husband and I discuss what's in those notebooks. He has his suspicions, I'm sure. Johnny was his best friend, after all. But if you never say the truth out loud, then does it actually count?

"I've known him…" she replies. "Let's see."

I watch her as she tallies things up. She chews at her bottom lip and it reminds me so much of another young woman sitting in that same spot, all those years ago. "Wait. I got it. Coming up on a year now." She smiles. "Ten months, four days and roughly eighteen hours, to be exact."

She brushes a crumb from the tablecloth into her hand. "Davis is amazing."

"Seems risky, meeting a man in prison."

"Yeah, it was." I'm not expecting her to say anything more, but when she opens her mouth, words come spilling out. She speaks like she's rehearsed what she has to say, like she's afraid she's not going to get to say her piece unless she says it in a hurry. "It was crazy, really. But a friend of mine came to stay here, and she told me all about it—mostly about it being haunted. Then I was curious, so I looked the story up… I love true crime—it's funny because I think I remember hearing about it when it happened. But I was young, you know?"

You're still young. I smile and it's like déjà vu. Nothing ever changes.

She waves a hand in the air. "So I wrote to him."

"You wrote to him?" I think of Shelby and I wonder how such a thing can happen. "You just looked up a man in prison and decided to become pen-pals?"

"Well, it wasn't exactly like *that.*" She giggles. "I didn't expect to fall in love. I guess I just really wanted to know him." She looks up at me. "Does that make sense?"

It does, and it doesn't. But what an explanation of love, if I've ever heard one. *I guess I just really wanted to know him.* "Your parents can't be too happy," I say. "Do they know where you are?"

"They're livid. But they'll come around, eventually. You know how it is." She watches as I wipe down the table and fill the dishwasher. When I look over at her, she's staring at her fingernails. "In the meantime, Davey said we could hang out at his place." She raises her brow. "And so, here we are."

A tight smile fixes itself on my face. When it fades, I swallow hard. "And so, here you are."

A NOTE FROM BRITNEY

Dear Reader,

I hope you enjoyed reading *Passerby*.

Writing a book is an interesting adventure, it's a bit like inviting people into your brain to rummage around. *Look where my imagination took me. These are the kind of stories I like...*

That feeling is often intense and unforgettable. And mostly, a ton of fun.

With that in mind—thank you again for reading my work. I don't have the backing or the advertising dollars of big publishing, but hopefully I have something better...readers who like the same kind of stories I do. If you are one of them, please share with your friends and consider helping out by doing one (or all) of these quick things:

1. Visit my review page and write a 30 second review (even short ones make a big difference).

(http://britneyking.com/aint-too-proud-to-beg-for-reviews/)

Many readers don't realize what a difference reviews make but they make ALL the difference.

2. Drop me an email and let me know you left a review. This way I can enter you into my monthly drawing for signed paperback copies.

(hello@britneyking.com)

3. Point your psychological thriller loving friends to their free copies of my work. My favorite friends are those who introduce me to books I might like. **(http://www.britneyking.com)**

4. If you'd like to make sure you don't miss anything, to receive an email whenever I release a new title, sign up for my new release newsletter.

(https://britneyking.com/new-release-alerts/)

Thanks for helping, and for reading my work. It means a lot.

Britney King

Austin, Texas

July 2021

ABOUT THE AUTHOR

Britney King lives in Austin, Texas with her husband, children, two very literary dogs, one ridiculous cat, and a partridge in a peach tree.

When she's not wrangling the things mentioned above, she writes psychological, domestic and romantic thrillers set in suburbia.

Without a doubt, she thinks connecting with readers is the best part of this gig. You can find Britney online here:

Email: hello@britneyking.com
Web: https://britneyking.com
Facebook: https://www.facebook.com/BritneyKingAuthor
Instagram: https://www.instagram.com/britneyking_/
BookBub: https://www.bookbub.com/authors/britney-king
Goodreads: https://bit.ly/BritneyKingGoodreads

Happy reading.

ACKNOWLEDGMENTS

Many thanks to my family and friends for your support in my creative endeavors.

To the beta team, ARC team, and the bloggers, thank you for making this gig so much fun.

Last, but not least, thank you for reading my work. Thanks for making this dream of mine come true.

I appreciate you.

ALSO BY BRITNEY KING

Passerby

"Roils with passion, rancor, and greed wrapped in Southern politesse...
King's intricately woven mystery is sure to please fans of the thriller and
suspense genre far and wide."

Kill Me Tomorrow

A mind-bending thriller that's soaked with raw sensuality, as an
investigator's search takes a wicked turn when he meets a beautiful and
provocative woman.

Savage Row

A suspenseful thriller that very well could be set in the house next door.

The Book Doctor

A riveting new thriller about a writer desperate to make a comeback who
realizes the price of success when a stranger arrives at his door.

Kill, Sleep, Repeat

An intense and deadly provocative thriller which follows a woman who,
in a fight for survival, realizes her job may cost more than it pays.

Room 553

Room 553 is a standalone psychological thriller. Vivid and sensual, Room
553 weaves a story of cruelty, reckless lust, and blind, bloody justice.

HER

HER is a standalone psychological thriller which covers the dark side of female relationships. But equally—it's about every relationship anyone has ever had they knew was terrible for them. It's for those of us who swam for the deep end anyway, treading water because it seemed like more fun than sitting on the sidelines. It's about the lessons learned along the way. And knowing better the next time. Or not.

The Social Affair | Book One

The Replacement Wife | Book Two

Speak of the Devil | Book Three

The New Hope Series Box Set

The New Hope Series offers gripping, twisted, furiously clever reads that demand your attention, and keep you guessing until the very end. For fans of the anti-heroine and stories told in unorthodox ways, *The New Hope Series* delivers us the perfect dark and provocative villain. The only question—who is it?

Water Under The Bridge | Book One

Dead In The Water | Book Two

Come Hell or High Water | Book Three

The Water Series Box Set

The Water Trilogy follows the shady love story of unconventional married couple—he's an assassin—she kills for fun. It has been compared to a crazier book version of Mr. and Mrs. Smith. Also, Dexter.

Bedrock | Book One

Breaking Bedrock | Book Two

Beyond Bedrock | Book Three

The Bedrock Series Box Set

The Bedrock Series features an unlikely heroine who should have known better. Turns out, she didn't. Thus she finds herself tangled in a messy, dangerous, forbidden love story and face-to-face with a madman hell-bent on revenge. The series has been compared to Fatal Attraction, Single White Female, and Basic Instinct.

Around The Bend

Around The Bend, is a heart-pounding standalone which traces the journey of a well-to-do suburban housewife, and her life as it unravels, thanks to the secrets she keeps. If she were the only one with things she wanted to keep hidden, then maybe it wouldn't have turned out so bad. But she wasn't.

Somewhere With You | Book One

Anywhere With You | Book Two

The With You Series Box Set

The With You Series at its core is a deep love story about unlikely friends who travel the world; trying to find themselves, together and apart. Packed with drama and adventure along with a heavy dose of suspense, it has been compared to The Secret Life of Walter Mitty and Love, Rosie.

In the tradition of *Gone Girl* and *Behind Closed Doors* comes a gripping, twisted, furiously clever read that demands your attention, and keeps you guessing until the very end. For fans of the anti-heroine and stories told in unorthodox ways, *The Social Affair* delivers us the perfect dark and provocative villain. The only question—who is it?

A timeless, perfect couple waltzes into the small coffee shop where Izzy Lewis works. Instantly enamored, she does what she always does in situations like these: she searches them out on social media.

Just like that—with the tap of a screen— she's given a front row seat to the Dunns' picturesque life. This time, she's certain she's found what she's been searching for. This time, she'll go to whatever lengths it takes to ensure she gets it right—even if this means doing the unthinkable.

Intense and original, The Social Affair is a disturbing psychological thriller that explores what can happen when privacy is traded for convenience.

What readers are saying:

"Another amazingly well-written novel by Britney King. It's every bit as dark, twisted and mind twisting as Water Under The Bridge...maybe even a little more so."

"Hands down- best book by Britney King. Yet. She has delivered a difficult writing style so perfectly and effortlessly, that you just want to worship the book for the writing. The author has managed to make murder/assassination/accidental- gunshot- to-the-head- look easy. Necessary."

"Having fallen completely head over heels for these characters and this author with the first book in the series, I've been pretty much salivating over the thought of this book for months now. You'll be glad to know that it did not disappoint!"

Praise

"If Tarantino were a woman and wrote novels... they might read a bit like this."

"Fans of Gillian Flynn and Paula Hawkins meet your next obsession."

"Provocative and scary."

"A dark and edgy page-turner. What every good thriller is made of."

"I devoured this novel in a single sitting, absolutely enthralled by the storyline. The suspense was clever and unrelenting!"

"Completely original and complex."

"Compulsive and fun."

"No-holds-barred villains. Fine storytelling full of mystery and suspense."

"Fresh and breathtaking insight into the darkest corners of the human psyche."

THE SOCIAL AFFAIR

BRITNEY KING

COPYRIGHT

Hot Banana Press

Cover Design by Britney King LLC

Cover Image by Mario Azzi

Copy Editing by Librum Artis Editorial Services

Proofread by Proofreading by the Page

First Edition: 2018

ISBN 13: 978-1979057455

ISBN 10: 1979057451

britneyking.com

To those who've walked into our lives without first asking permission...

PROLOGUE

Attachment is an awfully hard thing to break. I should know. I surface from the depths of sleep to complete and utter darkness. I don't want to open my eyes. I have to. "I warned you, and I warned you," I hear his voice say. It's not the first time. He called out to me, speaking from the edge of consciousness, back when I thought this all might have been a dream. It's too late for wishful thinking now. This is his angry voice, the one I best try to avoid. My mind places it immediately. This one is reserved for special occasions, the worst of times.

I hear water running in the background. Or at least I think I do. For my sake, I hope I'm wrong. I try to recall what I was doing before, but this isn't that kind of sleep. It's the heavy kind, the kind you wake from and hardly know what year you're in, much less anything else. I consider how much time might have passed since I dozed off. Then it hits me.

"You really shouldn't have done that," he says, and his eyes come into focus. Those eyes, there's so much history in them; it's all still there now. I see it reflected back to me. I read a quote once that said... a true mark of maturity is when someone hurts you, and you try to understand their situation instead of trying to hurt them back. This seems idealistic now. I wish someone had warned me. Enough of that kind of thinking will get you killed.

"Please," I murmur, but the rest of what I want to say won't come. It's probably better this way. I glance toward the door, thinking about what's at stake if I don't make it out of here alive, wondering whether or not I can make a break for it. It's so dark out—a clear night, a moonless sky. The power is out, I gather, and it's a fair assumption. This has always been one of his favorite ways to show me what true suffering is like. That alone would make an escape difficult. I would have to set out on foot and then where would I go? Who would believe me?

"You have it too easy," he says, as though he wants to confirm my suspicions. "That's the problem nowadays. People consume everything, appreciate nothing."

He lifts me by the hair and drags me across the bedroom. I don't have to ask why. He doesn't like to argue where he sleeps, where we make love. It's one of our safe spaces, but like many things, this too is a facade. Nothing with him is safe.

"You like your comforts, but you forget nothing good comes without sacrifice."

"I haven't forgotten," I assure him, and that much is true. Sacrifice is something I know well.

He shakes his head, careful to exaggerate his movements. He wants the message he sends to sink in. "I don't know why you have to make me so angry."

I glance toward the window, thinking I see headlights, but it's wishful thinking. Then I reach up and touch the wet spot at the crown of my head. I pull my hand away, regretful I felt the need for confirmation. Instinct is enough. If only I'd realized this sooner. I didn't have to put my fingers to it to know there would be blood; the coppery scent fills the air. "It's not too bad," he huffs as he slides one hand under my armpit and hauls me up. "Come on," he presses, his fingertips digging into my skin. "Let's get you stitched up."

I follow his lead. There isn't another option. Head wounds bleed a lot, and someone's going to have to clean his mess up. If I live, that someone will be me. *This is how you stop the bleeding.* "What time is it?"

"Oh," he says, half-chuckling. "There's no need to worry about that. She's already come and gone."

I don't ask who he's referring to. I know. Everything in me sinks to the pit of my stomach. It rests there and I let it. I don't want him to see how deeply I am affected by what he's done. It's more dangerous if I let it show. But what I want to happen and what actually does, are two very different things. I know because my body tenses, as it gives over to emotion until eventually it seizes up completely. I don't mean for it to happen. It has a habit of betraying me, particularly where he is concerned. Your mind may know when something's bad for you. But the body can take a little longer. He knows where to touch me. He knows what to say. Automatic response is powerful, and like I said before, attachment is hard to break.

He shoves me hard into the wall. I guess I wasn't listening. I shouldn't have made a habit of that either. I don't feel the pain. I don't feel anything. "Ah, now look what you made me do," he huffs, running his fingers through his hair. He's staring at me as though this is the first time he's seeing me. His face is twisted. He wants me to think he's trying to work out his next move. He isn't. He's a planner, through and through.

Still, he's good at concealing what he doesn't want anyone to know. If only I'd been more like that. I wasn't. That's why I don't know if this is it, if this is the end. I only know where it began.

"We had an agreement," he reminds me. And he's right.

We did have an agreement.

That's how this all started.

READ MORE HERE: https://books2read.com/thesocialaffair